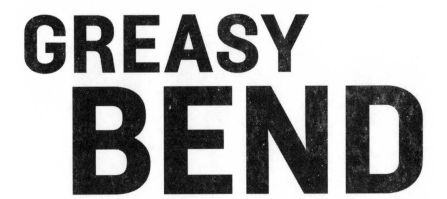

GREASY
BEND

KRIS
A NOVEL
LACKEY

BLACK
STONE
PUBLISHING

Printed in the United States of America

First edition: 2019
ISBN 978-1-4708-1408-3
Fiction / Mystery & Detective / Police Procedural

1 3 5 7 9 10 8 6 4 2

CIP data for this book is available
from the Library of Congress

Blackstone Publishing
31 Mistletoe Rd.
Ashland, OR 97520

www.BlackstonePublishing.com

To Joel Morgan
Michael Carr
and
Mary Bess Whidden

CHAPTER 1

Hannah Bond had just crossed the Washita River bridge on Oklahoma 1 when she saw a thin man standing at the barbed-wire fence that separated a vivid green stand of winter wheat from the highway's brown right-of-way. He waved his arms over his head. Bond pulled her cruiser onto the shoulder. As she set the brake and switched on the cruiser's strobes, she quickly scanned the field for idled farm machinery. Not so many years ago, these flag-downs often meant ugly accidents. Now, most farmers had cell phones. All she saw was a gray-and-red 1950s Ford row crop tractor parked by the fence, spouting gray exhaust. She also saw its tire tracks in the wheat. It had come straight across the field from the river.

Two steps down the embankment, she recognized Mason Arterbury by his violet cheeks and woolly white brows. Against the cold north wind, he wore Carhartt coveralls and a burnt-orange knit cap that twisted up like a flame.

Arterbury windmilled an arm to hurry Bond. He failed.

As she neared, he pointed toward the river. "Deputy, ma'am, there's a dead body hung up in a cottonwood snag, just at the end of Greasy Bend."

"I'll drive down to Mockingbird and follow the river back up.

You park your tractor where you want me to stop."

Arterbury nodded, wide-eyed as a toddler. He mounted his tractor, clutched it into gear, and slapped the hand throttle. A vapor of sleet wafted into a rank of bur oaks at the field's edge.

Bond radioed the Johnston County Sheriff's dispatcher in Tishomingo, county seat and former capital of the Chickasaw Nation, and eased her cruiser along the riverside trail. The understory of hackberry and sumac thrashed in the wind. The sky darkened, and a denser wave of sleet shushed against her windshield. The riderless tractor appeared. Bond put on a brown aviator hat and buckled the earflaps under her chin. Then she pocketed her phone and pulled gloves on.

As Bond neared the tractor, Arterbury's torso bobbed up above the bank's rim. Apparently, he had gone back down to the river to make sure the dead body had stayed put. When he met Bond on the road, he looked up at her. "Yore tall. I forgot," he said.

"Lead the way," she said.

At the lip of the bank, he pointed down. "It's steep, but it ain't far."

They grasped oak-root banisters as they heel-slid down red Permian mud. The Washita swirled around red clots of flotsam. The clouds briefly thinned, spilling crooked light. Arterbury palmed a shock of willow branches aside to reveal the white grimace of an elderly woman, her gray eyes fixed on the hidden sun. A fork of cottonwood had caught one ankle. The other was missing.

"Somethin's got at her," Arterbury said. "Coyotes, prob'ly."

The woman's plum knit trousers ballooned clownishly, and her black blouse wrapped her neck like a scarf. Livid mastectomy scars tracked her chest, and her silt-stained bra rode under her arms, its prostheses lost. The body was slightly tilted in the snag, and Bond could see the small hands, bound in the back by quarter-inch sisal rope. Suddenly, the physical details flew together. Bond's gaze snapped to the racked face. She inhaled sharply and blinked.

"It *is* her, ain't it? The Nazarene. Germans. From over Wapanucka."

A gust of wind caught the upper limbs of the snag, and the corpse shuddered.

Hannah fought the urge to unzip her uniform coat. In her mind, the dead could feel. "Lang. Alice."

"You seen the bullet hole by her ear?"

"Yeah."

Sirens whooped out across the wheat. Bond shook her head. Monkeyshines. The state Medical Examiner's Office in Oklahoma City was a long drive, and nothing was happening on Greasy Bend until an ME investigator got here.

Two days earlier Hannah Bond and Alice Lang had filled freezer bags at the Church of the Nazarene food bank in Tishomingo. Alice had opened a crate of frozen hot dogs from the regional bank and gasped, turning the label of one package toward Hannah. Everything on it except the brand name, Flying T Ranch, was printed in Cyrillic script. Alice said, "What kind of writing is that? Outer Mongolian? I'll swan, you never think of our weenies making their way to the ends of the earth."

Arterbury said, "She worked for the Indians."

"Chickasaw Nation," Bond said. "She was an accountant at Paska Manufacturing in Marietta. They precision-machine parts for baggage conveyors. Retired last year."

"I thought the Langs was German."

"You don't have to be Chickasaw to work for the nation, but I think she had a Turner up in the tree."

After Alice retired, she had gone with Hannah a few times to the outlet mall across the Texas line in Gainesville. Not a month had passed since they drove to Ardmore to hear the baby-faced John Fullbright sing "Jericho." As they were leaving the little civic theater, Alice said, "That young man …"

"*Oh,* yeah," Hannah said.

Again the clouds massed and lowered. A driving sleet crept down the valley and did not stop when it found the corpse of Alice Lang. Bond watched the ice fill her surgical wounds and cover her eyes. Arterbury clambered up the bank to meet the posse. Bond looked upriver and pinched her brow.

CHAPTER 2

Bill Maytubby steered his Chickasaw Lighthorse Police cruiser around Tishomingo's square, which commanded a bluff above Pennington Creek. In the square's center rose the stately former Chickasaw Nation Capitol, built of local Pennington granite. Sleet curtained its silver cupola and snapping flag

Maytubby approached the twenty-first-century seat of civil government, the Johnston County Courthouse. It was squat and dull as a salt lick. No sooner had he passed it than sheriff's cruisers spooled from the lot, sirens pitching up. He pulled over to let them pass. Hannah Bond might know what the commotion was about. He would call her after lunch.

Maytubby turned off Main into the chat parking lot of Gonzalez Mexican Restaurant. Simple white concrete-block building, acrylic sign with the compulsory green and red peppers. He had long ceased to see the building or the sign. He scented the hand-battered chile rellenos eased into fresh hot oil.

He looked for Jill Milton's mystic-green Accord, which he found nosed into a slot on the restaurant's lee side. She would have gone in through the kitchen to escape the wind. He always came through the kitchen, to watch the owner fillet Big Jims and stuff them with queso blanco. Today, the owner noticed Maytubby and nodded toward the east side of the dining room. The gesture was more handshake than help, because Maytubby and his fiancée always sat at the same window table if it was free, so they could look out over a clear pool of Pennington Creek.

A waiter at that table blocked his view of Jill Milton. Maytubby was surprised to see him setting plates of steaming rellenos on the gingham oilcloth. When the waiter left, Maytubby took his place. Jill was settling her raspberry squall jacket in the chair next to the window.

"So," Maytubby said.

Jill spun around, her important black hair turning a veronica.

Maytubby held his Smokey hat in both hands and nodded at the table. "He has good taste."

"Don't sound so surprised."

"I imagined him as a burrito man."

"Of course you did. That's what got you the boot. You think everybody but you is a burrito man."

"I'm overweening, is what you're saying."

"Your rellenos are getting cold, is what I'm saying, Sergeant. What's all the Keystone business out there?" She cocked her head toward the street.

"Don't know. Wasn't on that frequency. I'll call Hannah after lunch." Maytubby laid his hat on the window chair and unzipped his uniform coat. "First time you've ordered ahead. Does this mark a new frontier in the relationship?"

"What else have you ever ordered here?"

"I might have felt like something different today."

"Like what?"

"Oh, I don't know. Burrito."

"Cold rellenos are nasty." She pointed her fork at his plate, and they both ate quickly.

When they paused for water, she said, "I ordered ahead because I've got a two o'clock in-service with the dietary staff at CNMC."

"Do any of your patients get chile rellenos?"

"Do they get chile rellenos. Chile rellenos are the backbone of medical nutrition."

"I knew it."

Maytubby noticed the little keloid scar on the bridge of Jill's nose. The summer before, a murderer named Hillers broke her nose on the gas tank of his motorcycle before Hannah Bond separated him from that motorcycle. Hillers was doing life in McAlester, a slug from Hannah's disreputable old .38 nestled against his femur.

Jill lifted the last remnant of the chile by its stem and finished it off. Maytubby did the same. They stared down at sleet falling into Pennington Creek. A few miles downstream, red Washita silt would stain its clear aquifer water like blood in a bath.

"Where were you ambushing the scourge Sugar this morning?"

"Thackerville."

"A ravaged city, I hear."

"Tumbrels and pyres."

"Then the Eagle nutrition troupe rides out of the east, sunlight glinting off its silver Chickasaw Nation Suburban, brass fanfare from the heavens."

"I need to put that part in the grant next year. Where it said 'reducing the incidence of type two diabetes.'"

"Might make USDA uneasy. They'll cut your fake-vegetable budget."

"Speaking of, the girl who played Rain That Dances in the Eagle play?"

"The one who carries the veggie basket and says something about trying different colors every day."

"This morning, she tipped the basket and spilled a plaster tomato on the stage. It broke in a million pieces. Big cloud of plaster dust. One kid yelled, 'They want us to eat glass!' This other kid screamed, 'Rain That Dances dropped a tomato bomb!' It was bedlam."

"I see a casting call for Rain That Dances."

"No, she stuck it out, but she had the trembly lip. Where were you meting out rough justice this morning?"

"Checkerboard allotment lands on Oil Creek between Drake and Nebo. Cattle rustlers."

Dishes clattered in the kitchen.

"Did you hang 'em high?" Jill said.

"We—Murray County sheriff and I—don't know who's doing it. Owner and the guys he suspects are all members of the nation. All we got are tire and boot tracks. Get this: The pickup truck and cattle trailer together have eight tires. None of them match. No two alike."

"What about the boot tracks?"

"Umm. If you had gone to policeman school like me, you wouldn't ask a question like that."

"You know, medical nutrition has a special diet to treat people like you."

"Overweening people."

"Yeah."

"What's on it?"

"Wiener schnitzel and bananas." She picked up her jacket and pushed her chair back. "Some dude almost rear-ended me on Thirty-Two, around Lebanon, when I was on my way down a couple hours ago. Big honkin' Supercab. I was doing sixty-five, and he whipped around me like I was a slalom gate."

"Late for his pedicure at the Super Walmart."

"'S'what I'm thinkin'. We caravaning back to our nation's capital?" They left bills on the table and stood.

Maytubby put on his campaign hat. "I have to deliver a subpoena in Madill."

Outside, they stood under the eaves while sleet danced on the car hoods. Jill drew her head back and put her hands on her hips. "You can't say lame shit like that when you're wearing that hat." She snatched it off his head and put it on. It slid down to the little scar. She lifted her arm and pointed to the sky. "Saddle my mount, Corporal! Tonight when I have slain the rogue grizzly that has terrorized the citizens of Skagway, they will enjoy the peace that has so long eluded them!"

He peeled the hat away and kissed her.

CHAPTER 3

Maytubby had just checked the subpoena address and pulled his black Charger onto Main when his radio crackled to life. "Bill?"

"Hey, Sheila."

"You in Madill?"

"Tish."

"Tom Hewitt was shot at the Golden Play Casino in Wilson. Few minutes ago." Maytubby switched on his strobes. There was a little lag until the news struck. And after it did, he could hear Sheila's voice in the air but not attend it. He kicked the cruiser over the Washita and saw but didn't see a congregation of emergency vehicles on its bank.

Tommy Hewitt was a young prodigy on the stickball field. Quick, agile, freakishly intuitive. In a full sprint, he could swing his sticks back and snatch a ball over his shoulder. He laughed when he caught the ball, and he laughed when he was laid out by a chop block. He played with a giddiness that infected his teammates and demoralized his opponents. His dense ash-blond curls stood out on the field, and since he often possessed the ball, most of the kids just chased Tommy. They called his hair a Chickafro. The curls testified to the race-blindness of love in the old Indian Territory. His forebears were Lithuanian, Chickasaw, freed Chickasaw slaves. The Lithuanian was a coal miner.

At the Kullihoma stomp grounds, Maytubby had watched Tommy Hewitt bolt from a dusty scrum with the ball, the *towa,* pinched between the tiny baskets at the ends of his sticks. He broke two tackles and tagged the goalpost on the fly. Maytubby admired him and was surprised when the young man—then in high school—wanted to practice with him on weekday afternoons. They had been friends ever since.

Unlike Maytubby, Hewitt kept at the sport—*to'li'.* In the years when he was taking courses in electrical tech at Gordon Cooper in Shawnee—while he rose from apprentice to journeyman to licensed electrician, all along working for the nation—he played with Chikasha To'li'. In July, Tommy Hewitt had led the team in a long run in the World Series of Stickball in Philadelphia, Mississippi.

"Bill? Sergeant Maytubby? You still there?"

The sounds of the earth returned. He blinked, looked at his speedometer: 115. He pulled his foot off the accelerator. "Sheila, sorry."

"I'll back up. I know you were friends with him."

"Were. That means he's dead. Am I looking for a vehicle?"

"You did check out. You're probably halfway to Wilson."

Maytubby hit his brakes and pulled onto the shoulder. Anything but that. "Fox said me?"

"He said you were closer to him than anybody else in the Lighthorse. You know where he lives, right?"

"Yeah. Mill Creek."

"I'm sorry, Bill."

Maytubby made a U-turn and headed back toward Tishomingo. "What happened at the casino?"

"We don't know everything yet, but we do know that some guys dressed like casino security, caps pulled down real low, met the nation armored car. While they were robbing it out back, Tommy came out the rear door of the convenience store to add a circuit to the box. Spooked one of the perps. Guy shot him real close with the car guard's service pistol. In the heart."

"Oh." Maytubby couldn't think what else to say to the dispatcher.

He saw that the road had not frozen. His dash thermometer read 33. Still he slowed for the bridges. He had last seen Tommy and Nichole three weeks ago, when they hired a babysitter for their young daughters and met him and Jill in Ada for dinner at Papa Gjorgjio's. While they were waiting for their dinners to come, Tommy laid his phone on the table and played a video of his youngest dancing to Spike Jones' "Hotcha Cornia." She squealed and bugged out her eyes when the goat bleated. Tommy shoulder-danced to the music and played hambone on the table.

This time when he came upon the strobes flickering down on the Washita, he saw them. He didn't want to imagine Nichole's face a half hour from now. By the time Hannah Bond answered her cell, Maytubby had crossed the river and left the scene behind.

"Bill. That you just passed on One?"

"Yeah. You got a drowning?"

"It's Alice Lang."

"Your *friend* Alice Lang?" He winced at his own idiocy.

"Y—"

"Of course it's your friend. That's bad."

Bond was silent a few seconds. She cleared her throat. "I don't think she drowned. Gunshot wound to the head."

Hannah and Maytubby had trained together at CLEET, the Council on Law Enforcement and Training peace officer academy in Ada, seven years before. Nobody could ever remember what the acronym stood for. The first week of the academy, in sultry late June, he had thought she was a rube. She lumbered, had crooked teeth, and said "ain't." But as the weeks passed, he saw that when she moved her eyes without moving her head, she was taking in much more than the others, including him. She asked harder questions based on credible but strange hypotheticals. She shot like Natty Bumppo, and she drove like Ben Collins. She did not need the class called Custody Control. He liked her pokerfaced jokes, which the instructors never got. When they graduated, Bond first in the class and Maytubby second, they were hanging together.

"I can't come back, Hannah. Tommy Hewitt was shot to death a half hour ago. I'm on my way to tell his wife."

"Got *damn* it."

"Walked into an armored-car robbery at the Golden Play."

"An electrician and an accountant. Regular people. Same day. It doesn't seem hardly possible."

"No." Maytubby heard some people talking behind Hannah. He didn't want her to hang up and leave him with the specter of Nichole, living the last few minutes of her life with Tommy Hewitt.

A white Crown Victoria approached from the north—no roof lights but definitely government. He checked its logo and told Hannah an ME investigator was ten minutes out.

"Fast," Hannah said. "I'm glad for that." Wind and sleet crackled through her voice.

"You're not in your cruiser. It's cold."

"Yeah."

Maytubby scanned ghostly dolomite outcrops shrouded in cold fog. "You can't leave Alice by herself."

"I sent ever'body up to the road. I don't want 'em looking at her."

"If it were you."

"Yeah. If it was me. The dead deserve privacy. People think it's a license to stare."

"I'm in Mill Creek, Hannah. I'll get back to you."

Maytubby turned east on Main and was out of town in two blocks. A train hauling quarry rock blocked him. It rumbled and squeaked. He broke a sweat. He had eaten at the Hewitts' table a dozen times, ridden the wild-haired girls horsey on his knees.

As he turned into the drive, which in summer was shaded by pecan trees, his gut fisted and his eyes got hot. The cruiser's tires popped pecan husks, spooking a crow from one of the naked branches. *Where late the sweet birds sang.* Maytubby had read the sonnets.

Sleet collected under the dead Bermuda grass. The cruiser's thermometer now read 32. He radioed Sheila and told her he was at the Hewitt house and would tell Nichole right away. As he parked in front of the 1970s red-brick ranch house, he saw Nichole peer through her kitchen window. His boots crunched on the flagstones, and a quarry whistle moaned like a wolf in the distance.

The front door opened, and Nichole stood behind the glass storm door. She was wiping her hands on a dish towel and smiling at him. Her strong nose, arch eyes, and small upper lip reminded him of a young Barbara Stanwyck. So did her dancer's posture. He resisted the urge to smile back, in fact looked sternly into her eyes. Her face fell, and her eyes grew large as she pushed open the door.

In the hall, Nichole took his elbow and turned him toward her. He couldn't hear any child sounds in the house. "Is it Jill or Tommy?" she whispered as she wrung the towel.

"It's Tommy."

"Bill, he's a master electrician!" she stage-whispered, to prove he was wrong.

"He wasn't electrocuted, Nichole."

Maytubby took her into the kitchen. On the way, she dropped the towel and began to tremble. He steadied her and pulled out a chair. The overhead light was off, and the winter light was dying quickly.

"There was an armored-car robbery at the Golden Play in—"

"Wilson, I know," she whispered. "He wired that whole site when it went up."

"Tommy went out back of the convenience store to work on the box."

"And he walked into it." She put her hand on her forehead as if she were going to be sick. "Oh, my sweet Jesus. No." Maytubby knelt by her chair as she pitched into shuddering sobs. She pressed her mouth against his shoulder so she would not wake her children.

CHAPTER 4

Cold arid wind buffeted the Lighthorse cruiser. Maytubby was driving into a low, brilliant winter sun. The sleet had ended just before Nichole's mother arrived from Tecumseh, rolling a large black suitcase behind her. She was prepared, as Nichole herself always was.

The children had never awakened. By the time he left the Hewitt house, Nichole was pale and spent, lying on the couch in front of a cold fireplace. A framed photo of the stickball team hung over the couch. A beaming Tommy Hewitt held a trophy above his teammates, who were smeared with dirt and blood. There had been no good time to call Jill, recount the day's red harvest. When he unmuted his cell, he saw she had called. So she knew.

He pushed the call button on his cell, put it on speaker, laid it on the console. As it rang, the medical examiner's sedan passed him going north to Oklahoma City. There might be another like it heading north from Wilson. "Are you with Nichole?" Jill said.

"I stayed until her mother came from Tecumseh."

"So is she in any shape I should talk to her?"

"Probably not. She's been crying for a long time. The kids were asleep. But Nichole's mother is like Nichole—head screwed on right. Calm."

"When calm is a possibility."

"Yeah."

"Bill, it's unthinkable. I heard about the robbery and murder on KCNP in my office ten minutes ago. I called Sheila, and she told me Fox had sent you to tell Nichole."

The phone fell silent while they thought of what remained to be said. A gust of wind jolted the cruiser.

"Did KCNP say the body of Hannah's friend Alice Lang was found on the Washita with a bullet wound to the head?"

"Yes. I mean, Alice *Lang*? A retired bookkeeper who worked in a food pantry? And Hannah Bond doesn't make friends at the drop of a hat. Childhood of betrayals, sister killed by her foster father. I know that was a long time ago, but it seems like she's being fate-bullied."

"I just crossed the Washita, and I see her cruiser is still there. The ME passed me going back to OKC. I'll stop down there and talk to her." They agreed to meet for a late dinner.

Bond wasn't in her cruiser. Maytubby stood outside the crime scene tape, which snapped and buzzed in the fierce wind. Small drifts of sleet crept around exposed bur oak roots. With his eye, he followed the tape down to the water's edge, where it framed a snag. Bond was not there. Though she would not be assigned to the investigation of Lang's murder, she wouldn't wait until tomorrow to begin it. He swapped his Smokey hat for a black watch cap and picked up his flashlight. He turned his back on the sun and walked upstream, into the wind.

Soon he wished he had put on gloves. He walked more than a mile, under the highway bridge and along a marsh. Evening sunlight turned the light bark of the tall cottonwoods neon orange. The trees creaked in the wind like rusted vanes. A barn owl glided through the thicket.

As Maytubby watched rushes flailing in the gathering dusk, he felt the chill of death, a pang of superstitious dread. The abating glow gave the land the cast of a lurid dream.

He almost walked past Hannah Bond. The wind erased his walking sounds, and she was knee-deep in the marsh, bent at the waist and shining her flashlight on a clump of cattails. Her aviator hat and brown uniform made her look like a downed pilot from the first war. Maytubby whistled between his fingers. She didn't turn around but raised her left hand, with the flashlight, to acknowledge the only person in her life who whistled at her. There was a brilliant stroke of light, and Maytubby realized both how dark it was and that Hannah was photographing something. When she turned to face him, the phone was already in some pocket. She waded toward him, her head high and tilted a little back, the way she held it when she was angry.

"One of her fake boobs," she said. "OSBI and Sheriff Magaw would have my head on a platter if I touched it. It'll be in Lake Texoma by midnight. Some peckerwood down there'll think it's his trotline."

She pulled on examination gloves and took a small plastic bag from her duty belt. From the bag, she snapped out an elastic object, held it to Maytubby's face.

It was a blue disposable glove, its index and middle fingers torn. "Found this before the fake boob. This can't go floating down to Texoma. It stays with me. I photographed it wrapped around a cattail."

As she rebagged the glove, Maytubby nodded. "Lot of riverbank for OSBI to sift tomorrow."

"Tomorrow won't be the start of it. At least it's wintertime—not so many folks going to the river." Bond turned and walked with Maytubby toward the cruisers. "Alice was afraid of water. She had a thing about long bridges. That Roosevelt Bridge across Lake Texoma gave her nightmares. When we went to the outlet mall in Gainesville, she made me drive over the Red. And she shut her eyes while I did."

"How did she get to the City? Can't do it without crossing the South Canadian."

"Alice tried to stay between rivers."

"Did something happen when she was young?"

Bond was silent a few beats. "She never said. And you know I don't ask."

"I do." He switched his flashlight on. When they had passed under the highway bridge, the blue strobes of her cruiser beat across the cold valley.

"This has been a day of shit, hasn't it, Bill?"

"Yes, it has, Hannah."

Her boots croaked as they struck the dry grama stalks. "Maggots," she said.

Maytubby and Bond said nothing else. They got in their cruisers and drove to higher ground.

CHAPTER 5

Maytubby and Jill Milton sat across from each other at a small drop-leaf table and ate in silence. A tapered candle in a ceramic bottle was the only light in the garage apartment. Once, the candlelight had alarmed a neighbor living in one of the thirties oil-boom mansions on King's Road, and he had called the Ada Fire Department. Maytubby's gable-and-wing across town, built when its address was Indian Territory, funneled too many drafts for winter dining. The garage apartment was caulked, at least. Its first tenant was Jill's great-grandfather John Milton, whose father was a Chickasaw freedman, a black man owned by a Chickasaw man. John Milton married a Chickasaw woman and chauffeured the millionaire who lived in the Tudor mansion up front.

Maytubby had cooked black beans and carrots with cumin and vinegar. Jill sautéed the rest of the carrots in butter and thawed basil. A single old-fashioned glass half full of Marietta Old Vine Red sat at the top of each plate. The large, dim room smelled sweet. On the evenings they spent together—most evenings—they read novels to each other or listened to *Fresh Air* or *This American Life* on KGOU-Ada. Sometimes, Jill played clawhammer banjo.

Tonight, the radio was off, and the novel they were reading, *The Book of Ebenezer Le Page,* about a curmudgeon on the Channel Island of Guernsey, lay unopened on an end table by the canvas couch. Maytubby's uniform coat and Jill's squall jacket hung from the backs of their chairs. The norther beat against the old clapboard and made the rafters snap.

Jill cleared her throat. "Nichole was still asleep when I called and talked to her mother. The kids were eating mac and cheese. They were asking about their daddy."

Maytubby shook his head, looked at his empty spoon. "And the answers they get will make no sense."

"Only what happens starting today."

"When the air that they breathed …"

"Yes." She looked down at her food and touched her upper lip. Below the King's Road bluff, a siren dopplered away on the State 3 bypass. "Can you go over there with me tomorrow night?"

"I think so."

"You don't know if Fox will put you on Tommy's case."

"I won't give him a choice."

"What about the rustlers?"

"They're rustlers. That also doesn't give Fox a choice."

"You can't solve your friend's murder, because you have to track down the guys who stole some cows."

"Exactly."

"You don't know if the shooter is an Indian or not. And if he's not, it's on the US attorney."

"That's what Fox might say, you mean?"

Jill nodded.

"I'll ask him how we'll know if the shooter is an Indian or not until we find him."

"You're going to ignore the rules anyway."

"*Mmnngg.*" He looked at her black eyes over the candle flame. They shone under a deep worry line. Maytubby felt a twinge of guilt when he recalled that the line appeared when they were making love. "Just division-of-labor rules."

"The candle reminds me of Papa Gjorgjio's."

"I was thinking the same thing. Tommy mugging to that ridiculous Spike Jones song. Breaking his kids up."

"If I put it out, that will be what happens starting today."

"Let it burn?"

"Let it burn."

Washing dishes, they looked out the window toward the south, down the valley of the Clear Boggy. Constellations of amber sodium lamps spun out to the horizon. In the clear, cold air, a gibbous moon cast enough light to make the land visible.

"One winter night," Jill said, "I had Ahloso Road to myself, and I drove with my lights out."

"The luster of midday."

"Yeah, 'the moon on the breast of the new-fallen snow.' I'm glad we can't see Mill Creek from here."

"The curvature of the earth is repressing it for us."

Maytubby dried the last dish and held it above his head. "It's hard to see dirt in candlelight."

Jill tapped at her laptop until a Café Noir song came from its tiny speakers. They liked the weird, calm fusion of old cowboy serenades and French cabaret music. She took his hand and led him to the small empty space in front of the couch. They held each other and slow-danced as the candle guttered.

* * *

Hannah Bond sat alone at the kitchen table in her frame postwar cottage on the north side of Tishomingo, drinking coffee from a mug that said, "Van's Pig Stand." The eastern sky had a little light in it. She watched delivery bobtails upshifting on their way out of town—Hiland Dairy, Ben E. Keith, Coca-Cola. The gas wall heater clanged on and beat a tattoo.

Bond still wore her uniform. After midnight, she had finally drifted to sleep in her recliner, only to start up minutes later. Television audiences laughed at late-night comics. She didn't hear what the comics were saying. She walked the floor the rest of the night, occasionally kicking a chair.

CHAPTER 6

Before dawn, Maytubby ran from Jill's apartment to the Chickasaw Nation Medical Center and back—six miles and change. In warm weather, in the daytime, he ran country trails barefoot, like the Tarahumara, whom he admired. On short winter days, when he had to run on shard-strewn roads in the dark, he wore gray New Balance runners and a Petzl headlamp.

After he had showered and dressed, Jill's cell alarm played a banjo tune, "Blackberry Blossom." When she stirred, he turned it off.

Maytubby scraped frost from his cruiser windshield with his Pontotoc County Library card. When he set off for the Golden Play in Wilson, the sun had just cleared the roofs of the King's Road mansions. His shift would begin in six hours, so he didn't have to think about Chief Fox. To make sure Fox didn't make a preemptive strike, he turned his police radio off.

Looking down on the Washita from the State 1 bridge a half hour later, he saw Hannah Bond's old Skylark in the frosted grass. She was making hay before Sheriff Magaw took her off the case and sent her to investigate livestock on the right-of-way.

In Ardmore, Amtrak's Heartland Flyer trundled above him on its way to Fort Worth, its buffed aluminum filling his cruiser with reflected light. Maytubby and Jill had boarded the Flyer once at Pauls Valley and ridden it to see a Caravaggio exhibition at the Kimball Museum in Fort Worth. The Flyer didn't so much fly as taxi on double track, waiting for a freight to pass.

US 70 was four-lane, and deserted as Maytubby drove through Lone Grove. The path of a rare winter tornado a few years earlier was still plain in the little town named for a desolate stand of cedars. The townspeople had thought a malfunction set off the storm sirens in February. One of the dead was a trucker whose rig was lifted off the highway.

A few miles of rolling country and then, on the outskirts of Wilson, Maytubby saw the Black and Gold Casino and the Wilson Travel Plaza. Both were Chickasaw Nation enterprises, and they shared a gabled building that was designed to look rustic. The sign on US 70 was a squat faux oil derrick, and the font was hillbilly.

The nation van that Tommy Hewitt drove was parked at the edge of a mostly empty lot. A decal of the nation's seal, with its purple band, was affixed to the driver's-side door. Crime scene tape, strung between signposts, fenced the van. Maytubby parked, ducked under the tape, and looked inside. It was spotless—no cups, not even a peanut shell on the seat. Though the van was a few years old, the cabin looked spanking new. It was clear Tommy had vacuumed the carpet. A small acrylic box in one of the cup holders contained an assortment of pens and mechanical pencils, all of them blue. Tucked in beside the box was a black-bound New Testament with some plastic bookmarks. Tommy was active Church of Christ. Maytubby was secular. They almost never talked about religion. The driver's visor was up because Tommy would have driven to work with the morning sun at his back. An elastic band around the visor held a recent 5 × 7 color photograph of his wife and children.

Maytubby walked to the rear of the building and saw that a large swath of the loading area was also taped off. In the middle of the pavement was a single small white pylon with the numeral "1" painted on it. A single casing. The low sun glinted off a few frozen puddles. The door of the electrical box Tommy Hewitt had been updating was still cracked open. Maytubby pulled out a pencil and opened the door all the way. He could see Tommy's handwriting beside the most recent breaker switches. The last he had identified was "WALK-IN 2." A red-ocher stain followed the lot's drainage slope and disappeared at a round drain grate.

Maytubby walked around the building and went in the front door of the little casino. A vortex of blue cigarette smoke spun in the sunlight of the open door. A very young security guard nodded at Maytubby and said, "Hey." Security guards were not, as a rule, commissioned officers.

Maytubby nodded. "Everett here?"

"Not usually at this hour, but since …"

"Yeah. Thanks."

Maytubby blinked in the sudden peripheral darkness. Only a few machines were playing their jaunty tunes, but dozens of high-def video screens blazed with color. Soon, he came to a door marked SECURITY. He entered and found Everett Briggs, the casino's chief of security, bent over a laptop screen, drinking coffee from a paper cup. Briggs looked up.

"Hell of a thing, Bill." He looked back down at the screen and shook his head. "Guard who sits here was in the john when it happened. He got grilled. Will."

Maytubby rounded the desk and stood beside Briggs. They were watching security camera footage of a nation armored car and a few men in Chickasaw Nation security guard uniforms. The camera was mounted on the roof of the building. None of the uniformed men's faces were visible. All were hidden by uniform caps, bills pulled low, and sunglasses. A flash of cheek showed a dark patch on one man's skin. Maytubby made Briggs go back and freeze the video. Maytubby pointed. "A black triangle inked or stuck on his face. Foils photo recognition. In case the low caps don't work."

"Driver, shotgun, back guard—no one said anything about it."

Briggs went back to just a few seconds before the arrival of the armored car. A late-model white Ford F-150 Supercab with a black, heavy-duty grille guard pulled slowly around the corner of the building into the back lot. Sleet whipped around the building's edges and over its roof. The pickup was spattered with mud.

"There," Briggs said. "White, of course."

"The 'medium build' of vehicles."

Three uniformed men wearing sidearms—the front passenger and two from the back—got out of the pickup and walked quickly toward the locked back door of the casino. One, the pickup's shotgun, was short, one middle height, and one very tall—maybe six-seven. They wore tight black driver's gloves. That looked odd, but the sleet and wind made it look less odd. They also wore dark athletic shoes—not regulation, but inconspicuous. When the armored car appeared and neared the casino's back door, the three men, hunched against the building funnel of cold wind, milled near the back wall, a dozen feet to the side of the door. They waved at the armored car's driver. A guard and the "hopper," the one who handles the cash, got out of the armored car and walked toward the door. The hopper was a woman. The bogus guards again waved at them, and the video showed the guard and the hopper nodding at them. The hopper and guard went inside, a real guard holding the door for them from the inside. The real guard's face didn't break the plane of the wall. The driver and his shotgun sat in the cab. They could not be seen on the video.

When the door was opened from the inside, again by a real security guard, the hopper and her guard came out of the building. When the door shut, the impostors walked up to them and appeared to chat them up. The real guard points to the other's face. He's maybe asking about the black triangle.

The turn of events was so quick, Maytubby could hardly follow it. One of the bogus guards, the tall one, grabbed the armored-car guard's pump shotgun, the short one yanked his pistol out of its holster, and the middle-height guy clumsily maced the hopper and took two bags of cash from her. The shotgun thief and the money guy bolted for the pickup. Before the little pistol thief took even a full step, he spun on his heel and aimed the pistol toward the right of the screen. Tommy Hewitt was outside the camera's field.

The pistol thief fired one shot and bolted for the pickup. The shotgun thief threw the gun on the pavement, and he and the money thief floundered into the pickup's bed. Only then did the driver and the passenger guard open their doors and draw their sidearms.

The shooter dropped his gun on the asphalt as well, just before he fence-jumped the side of the pickup bed. Smoke rose from the spinning rear tires of the pickup as it did a doughnut. The three fake guards were invisible in the bed. Never was there a clear view of the pickup's driver, though he had hairy hands. The license plate had been removed, no dealer sticker. Flame and smoke leaped from the armored-car driver's pistol, but only once before the tailgate of the getaway vehicle vanished behind the casino wall. It was not clear whether the shot had struck the pickup. The driver and his guards holstered their pistols, then ran off the bottom right of the scene, where Hewitt lay dying—or dead.

Briggs sped up the video—casino guards piling out the back door, fishtailing cruisers from Oklahoma Highway Patrol and the Carter County sheriff, an ambulance. "Not much more," he said, clicking off the video and bringing up his screen saver—Hereford cattle on a hillside. "What do you see?"

Maytubby stared at the Herefords a few seconds. They had really curly hair. "That truck pulls a trailer pretty regularly—new truck but dents over the hitch. But the bed isn't used to haul livestock—no shit stains and no skinning where the cage poles would fit. Mud is light colored—and gritty. Not from the redbed. The short impostor, the shooter, is left-handed even though he wears his holster on the right. He has a pronate step—walks on the outsides of his heels. Skilled marksman, we can see that. Did you zoom his neck tat for the feds?"

"Some kind of goat-man. Evil red eyes. High-def is good."

"It have a woodie?"

"What?"

"The goat-man."

"Curved."

"It's a satyr. A mythical creature."

Briggs shrugged. "You say so. Who would paint a triangle on his face to fool the camera and not cover that tat?"

"Maybe a clever fellow. Could you Google 'temporary tattoos' and 's-a-t-y-r'?"

Briggs matched the design at the second site. Maytubby said to the screen, "Doesn't mean it's not permanent."

"Just that if it is, he's dumb as a ditch carp." Briggs returned to the security video.

Maytubby pointed to the screen. "The very tall impostor cares that his clothes fit. He shaves his neck, and he doesn't like to step in water. His sneakers are new and clean. He has a cold, and I can't see any hair below his cap. The middle-size guy is either poor or doesn't care about his looks, or both. His hair hasn't seen clippers in a long time, and it's oily. His whiskers are scraggly, and he's wearing Reeboks from ten years ago, maybe thrift store. And orange socks. Don't think the mastermind thought he needed to mention black socks in the memo."

"Here comes the IP camera in the armored car. Lower angle but less coverage." Briggs bent and moved the mouse around. The video filled the screen with gray light. As the pickup appears from behind the wall, the driver is visible, but he is pulling something down over his face. "We looked—it's a pirate mask."

"He's the pirate king."

As the armored car and the truck move toward each other, the pirate king's shotgun passenger yanks his fake uniform cap down over his face. He has average-size fingers and a softish chin. Even seated, he is much shorter than the pirate king. About the same age. Before he opens the cab door, he twists in his seat and jabs a black-gloved index finger, his left, in the pirate king's face. Maytubby sees now that he is not wearing driving gloves, which have a stylish strap at the wrist, but tactical duty search gloves—cop gloves—which are plainer and have a thin utilitarian elastic band at the wrist. Then Shotgun gets out and joins the other two fake guards. They wear the same duty gloves.

The same scene he has just watched from above plays out, but from this angle he notices that the short fellow's gait is a swagger, which may have something to do with his pronate step. He may be running the show—or at least the troops on the ground.

"Banty rooster," Briggs said.

When the action moved to the back of the armored car, Briggs switched cameras.

"Gold piping is missing on the fake uniforms," Maytubby said.

When Shotgun grabbed the guard's pistol with his left hand, paused, and spun to shoot Tommy Hewitt, a slightly larger swatch of the shooter's face flashed between sunglasses and collar. Wheat complexion, long upper lip, strong cheekbones. Ropy neck muscles. For a fraction of a second, when he grimaced as he pulled the trigger, he showed a row of cockeyed teeth. This last detail tipped something in Maytubby's memory, but the noise was faint and far down a dark hallway.

Briggs brought the Herefords back up on the screen.

Maytubby stared at the Herefords. "Any of those guys—I know you can't see their faces—remind you of anybody who worked here?"

Briggs stared at the screen saver, too. "Huh. I never thought about it." Now he looked left, down at the busy wine-colored carpet. His eyes moved and stopped and moved as if he were examining faces in a lineup. His head lolled, and again he said, "Huh," and looked back up at Maytubby. "The slob," he said. "The way he bobbed his head like a cow when he walked."

"Think you could pull up his picture?"

"If I could remember his name. It's been a while, and he wasn't here very long. Hold on. I'll ask Meg in the travel stop." Briggs laid his palm on top of his head while he waited on the intercom phone. "Meg, Everett. What was the name of that slobby kid who worked here a couple of years ago? Stinky? Couldn't match his socks?" Briggs moved his palm back and forth on his head. Then he made a fist and rapped his desk. "*Yeah.* Thanks." He hung up and said, "Lon Crum. He stole canned food from the convenience store. I showed Meg the pictures, and she fired him."

A few clicks, and they were looking at the face of a young man in his early twenties: mottled pale face, scraggly blond facial hair, blue eyes under drooping lids. His mouth was open.

Maytubby pointed at the computer. "Can I run him?"

"Be my guest."

Maytubby logged on and searched the name and the photo in all his databases. He memorized a vehicle registration and tag number for a red 1991 Ford Ranger. The only tribal place Crum appeared was in the nation's HR files. He wasn't a member of the nation. Maytubby memorized the address in Ada. "The nation didn't prosecute the theft. And otherwise, he looks, uh, unconvicted."

Briggs smiled. "Never will be clean."

"Could you print this mug?"

"Yeah."

"How many times you replay this robbery?"

"Huh. FBI and Carter County sheriff watched it half the night."

"What'd they say?"

"Nothin'. Just tapped shit into their laptops. Deputy had to leave for an hour to work a car-heifer accident in the sticks."

"You mean this is not the sticks?"

"The *sticks* sticks."

"A*ha*. You think the shooter looks like an Indian?"

Briggs spread his fingers and waggled his hand. "Eh. Can't see his eyes."

"Pickup look familiar?" Maytubby smiled.

Briggs shook his head, lowered it, and gave Maytubby the side-eye. "I'll get stopped ten times before I get home to Ardmore. My two brothers have the exact same truck. It's about a quarter of the vehicles in Carter County. Smart crook."

"Maybe he just always wanted to fit in."

"Huh."

"Thanks, Everett."

Maytubby put on his sunglasses in the dark of the casino. Even so, the sunlight outside was dazzling. He checked his watch and found that he had time to take a back way back to Lighthorse headquarters in Ada.

Witnesses had seen the pickup speed west on US 70. That wouldn't have lasted long. The robbery was too well planned. Likely either a safe house or a vehicle change somewhere in the *sticks* sticks. Maytubby was blessed with perfect geographic recall. The way some savants could describe what happened on some random Monday decades ago, Maytubby could follow, in his imagination, every road he had ever traveled. So fixed was his memory that when he encountered any change on later trips—a new building, a sapling grown into a large tree, a missing road sign—he felt vaguely disoriented and had to slow down. And afterward, his memory would never accept the changes. For this reason, he never rearranged the meager furniture in his house and hated it when Jill moved hers.

As the tonneau of his cruiser warmed, his mind's eye watched the pickup going west very fast, the heads of the impostor guards bobbing up into the Bernoulli vortices of sleet. Suddenly, the brake lights flashed; the truck swerved left through a median cut, then south a couple of miles, then back east. Whiskey Lane, Bullrun Road, Anshultz Road. The route began to get fuzzy. Before it blurred completely, though, he saw the pickup, now going north on a deserted stretch of Jehovah Road, slow and stop near a small bridge. The fake guards got out of the truck and began to take off their uniforms, which they had been wearing over other clothes. They had trouble because of the gloves but did not remove the gloves. One of the guards gathered up the uniforms, carried them down the embankment and under the bridge, and returned empty-handed. Maytubby recognized Caddo Creek, which entered the Washita just above Greasy Bend.

He left the cruiser running and jogged back inside the casino. He asked Briggs to replay the second video. Only a few seconds in, he saw bits of other collars and sleeves peeping out from the uniforms. Not the neat guy's. "They put on the uniforms over other clothes," he said. He touched the computer screen in a couple of places.

"Damn. You're right," Briggs said. "You got a snitch in the lot?" He laughed dryly.

*   *   *

On his way back to Ada, Maytubby skipped the first part of the pickup's imagined journey and drove east and then north to Jehovah Road. Twenty minutes later, as he neared the creek bridge, every bois d'arc tree and oil service road he passed was in place. Nothing made him feel disoriented. When he came to the bridge, he switched on his strobes, got out of the car, and heel-slid down the grade. Even in this cold, he could smell the creosote in the bridge timbers. In the stark shadows they made, he saw nothing but beer cans and dead leaves. He looked up and down the creek. Nothing.

CHAPTER 7

Hannah Bond sat across from Oklahoma State Bureau of Investigation agent Dan Scrooby in a black-and-white striped booth at Hamburger King in downtown Ada. They were drinking coffee, waiting for their orders. It was just past eleven, but country people who chored at 4 a.m. were already working on saucer-size cheeseburgers. The air was sharp with fried onions.

Scrooby was wearing khaki pants, a navy jacket with the OSBI star embroidered on his chest, and a Heckler & Koch P30 in a nonregulation Texas cross-draw belt holster. An open laptop with a USB antenna angled away from his right hand. As he waited for their burgers to arrive, he spread his meaty hands on the gray Formica tabletop and exhaled loudly. "Some of these young agents we got now, Hannah, I don't need to tell you. They can't work five minutes in a row without …" He air-texted. "I try to talk to them …" He shot a glance at his laptop screen. "They start groping their phones and looking around like they're in pain. 'Hey!' I say." Scrooby then whistled loudly with his tongue. Every head in the restaurant turned. "*That* gets their attention."

"I bet."

He exhaled a gust of discontent.

"Last night about dark," Hannah said, "I found one of Alice Lang's fake boobs in some water weeds about a half mile up the Washita from her body."

"Did you …"

"No. I took a picture of it and emailed it to you last night. It was gone this morning when I went back."

Scrooby frowned and squinted at his laptop. "Did the subject line have 'boob' in it?"

"That was the subject, so yeah."

"I thought it was spam. Just a sec. Okay. Got it. GPS, too. That's good. Listen, Hannah, Magaw's turned the investigation over …"

Bond was pulling her phone from her jacket pocket. She switched it on and turned the screen toward Scrooby. Before considering the phone, he stuck out his lower lip and looked at the ceiling for effect.

"It's a nine Luger casing on Greasy Bend Bridge. And no, I didn't touch it. It's wedged real good in a rusted truss seam below the driving surface. I think somebody thought they kicked it off the bridge."

"Send the picture to me. We'll have a look. Like I was saying, Sheriff Magaw has turned the investigation over to OSBI. I wanted to talk to you because you were a friend of the victim."

"Do you know where Greasy Bend Bridge is?"

"No." Scrooby turned in his seat and looked at the kitchen door. Then he looked at his watch.

"It's three river miles above where Alice Lang's body hung up. Old camelback steel bridge, long way from houses, closed to car traffic. Young people go to the dead-end approaches to drink and hook up. Gun nuts go there to shoot stuff against the bank. Lots of vehicle tracks in the sand, lots of casings, lots of shooting."

"Sounds crowded."

"Not after dark in a norther. And hardly anyone shoots from the middle of the bridge. And the casing was new. I leaned over and smelled it. Fresh."

A thin young man in a white apron slid their plates onto the table.

Scrooby leered at his chicken-fried steak and white gravy. Bond knew from the few lunches they had had through the years that he would not hear a word she said until he had finished his food. She also knew that she wouldn't have to wait long.

When he pushed aside his plate and blotted his lips with a paper napkin, Bond was taking her third bite of a double bacon cheeseburger. He slid his laptop in front of him. "How long have you known Alice Lang?"

"Six years or so, but we didn't start doing things together until three years ago." Scrooby typed with his index fingers. "Listen, I'll save you some time." He looked up. "No, you'll have to keep typing. Alice and I were not *girlfriend* girlfriends. She never married. I don't know anything about her sex life. She never talked about sex. She grew up outside Wapanucka, studied accounting at East Central in Ada, worked at some car dealerships before the Chickasaw Nation built that machining plant in Marietta. There was a Turner back in her family, and some Turners still own Indian allotments, but I didn't know if she was a member of the nation or if that got her the accounting job at the plant. It was better work than she'd ever had, and she stayed until she retired last year."

Scrooby belched softly and held up a hand. "Hold on." His wrists crossed like a pianist's as his index fingers socked the laptop keys. A minute later, they stopped. "Okay."

"To her—Alice—gambling was an abomination. That's the word she used. So I don't think she had a gambling problem. She was real generous, helped everyone in her extended family. Worked with me in the Nazarene food pantry in Tish. She didn't wear makeup or dye her hair. She told me she'd never had a traffic ticket. I believe that. She drove so slow, it made you crazy. She was afraid of water. Got panicky when she had to drive over long bridges.

"She walked in the country a lot, had got bit by some yard dogs. Her car was still in her drive in Wapanucka this morning. But I don't think she walked late at night. Once, at her house, I saw a twenty-two rifle behind her front door. Typical for the country. She never talked about guns. She paid off her house in Wapanucka ten years ago." Bond told Scrooby the address and gave him directions. Then she waited for him to catch up. "She was in her early fifties when she got cancer and had her boobs taken off. I wasn't around her much then. When I got to know her, she had a sense of humor about it, made jokes about her falsies going south."

The apron boy took Scrooby's plate. It was pretty clear the cop wasn't still working on that.

"The bills I saw around her house were the usual: utilities, insurance. Besides her Bible, I only saw copies of one magazine. She subscribed to *Time*, and she read it. She didn't have pets—hated the dirt they made."

Scrooby typed a while, stopped, looked at Bond. "That it?"

"Yep." She went back to her burger.

Scrooby shrugged and snapped his laptop closed. "I have your number." Bond nodded as he slid out of the booth, paid his ticket, and left Hamburger King.

CHAPTER 8

Unless Sheriff Magaw had received complaints about a specific stretch of highway, he allowed his deputies to replenish the county's coffers on any profitable stretch of road they chose. Bond usually mined a sycamore-shaded stretch of State 7 where it crossed the Blue River. The clear rapids and pools made her stop thinking. But today, she drove farther east to Wapanucka and pulled onto the right-of-way near a crook in the highway. Her cruiser was hidden in both directions. This spot was not the idyllic Blue, which drew plein air painters and well-heeled trout anglers from Dallas, but it paid out quicker than a fixed slot. It had the additional advantage of being very close to the house where Alice Lang's nephew—the one Bond hadn't mentioned to Scrooby—was currently squatting.

The sheriff had no official quota, but Bond filled her customary notion of it in less than two hours. She drove a mile north of town on State 48, then, when it crossed Delaware Creek, turned east onto a one-lane dirt road that wound in and out of eroded washes as it followed the creek. In the bar ditch, brambles had snared rusted appliances and moldy sofas.

Before she turned up the driveway, she sent Maytubby a text so at least one person would know where she had gone. A cell phone was easy to trash.

The mailbox at the end of the driveway was a small white plastic bucket nailed to a head post on a bed frame. The rest of the frame was out of the road. On the bucket, someone had drawn a crude pig's head in runny red paint. The eyebrows made it look sinister. Alice had shown Bond the driveway out the car window, but not the house at the end of it. Alice did not walk on this road.

The driveway cut through heavy brush as it descended toward the creek. The ruts were paved with flattened beer cans and household trash. Slowly the light faded under a thatch of bare wind-whipped limbs that hissed like insects.

The front yard, when she reached it, was a caked slough. A small Ford pickup with most of its lights smashed out and all its surfaces ravaged sat high atop a set of monster tires. Mud covered everything. Bond looked around the yard for a dog. No living dog, but two rusted log chains, staked to the ground.

Fifty years before, the small house had been built with architectural adornments common to middle-class homes in the suburbs: turned porch supports, scrolled fascia, plastic shutters with circle dingbats in the center. But time and tenants had not been kind to it. Ropes of dried mud had been slung against its walls by the truck's spinning tires. The crooked shutters glowered. A makeshift stovepipe poked out the roof and leaned toward the gable, leaking a thin stream of blue smoke. Lang's mongrel woodpile had never been visited by a saw. It looked like a giant crow's nest. An ax lay flat on the ground.

Bond had not seen Jeff Lang since she arrested him for assault in Connerville two years earlier. She knew from Alice that his frightened parents had driven to Tishomingo two years before that and convinced a judge known for denying divorces to issue a restraining order on their own son. Sometime after he got kicked out, Alice had found him sleeping against a dumpster behind Subway. She woke him, fed him, gave him some pocket money. She also offered to pay his rent for a tiny shotgun house if he would take the county mental health clinic for a spin. What Alice told Bond she had learned from helping her nephew: "I should have let sleeping dogs lie." He badgered her relentlessly—for food, clothes, money, bail, attorney fees. Beneath this running man's pleas gleamed an edge of menace. Not long before she was killed, Alice had told Bond she was considering baking the no-divorce judge a pecan pie.

Bond ducked out of her cruiser and walked around the truck to the door. The truck was too high to see into. She pounded loudly, took a step back, and laid her fingers on her holster. No sound from inside. She pounded again. This time she heard a loud expletive and something that sounded like breaking furniture. A few foot thumps, and the door flew open. A foul gust of old meat, oak smoke, and stale beer swept over her. Jeff Lang remained in shadow, panting. She said nothing.

"If it ain't the female bitch. You got nothin' on me now, so it must be some bug crawled up your ass."

"Did you know your aunt Alice died?"

Lang was silent for a few seconds before he said, "So? How's it your business?"

"She was a friend of mine."

In the dimness, Lang stuck out his lower lip and shook his head slowly. "You come all the way out here for a cry party and I'm fresh out of clean hankies." Then he cackled high, like a very old tenor.

"Did anyone tell you?"

"That sow *would* have you for a friend. You put me in jail, and she tried to put me in the crazy hospital. She already spoke evil of me to my parents. I heard her thu my wall.

"She won the first round. Round two, she followed me around; then when I needed some money, there she was with a wad of cash." Lang stepped out of his house into the wintry shade. He was about a foot shorter than Bond. He wore a threadbare yellow sweatshirt with the word JACKETS printed on it in red, black sweatpants, and cowboy boots. His head was shaved, and he wore a shaggy red Van Dyke. His hazel eyes glistened, and the vessels in his temples bulged. He extended a cupped hand toward Bond, miming the cash offering. "She wanted me to take it. Sure she did. You know why?"

Bond said nothing.

"You know why?"

"No."

"She wanted to get me in debt so she could make interest off me. A shitload. I was going to be her little cash machine."

"How much interest did she charge you?"

Jeff Lang glared at her. His head began to tremble, and his eyes teared up. He made fists and dropped them to belt level. "That's *neither* none of your fucking business! What are you doing here?"

"I just came to tell you your aunt had died."

"You done that. And you hear me say you brung me good tidings." He smiled and raised his arms as if he were cheering. His arms remained in the air as he spun on his heel, walked into the house, and kicked the door shut.

Bond walked backward toward her cruiser. Before she reached it, a savage, exultant scream from inside the house flushed sparrows from a yard tree. She was reminded of Jeff Lang's face when she was cuffing him for the assault. It was all crimson with blood except the whites of his eyes and then, when he laughed, his big yellow canines.

She opened the cruiser door slowly, using it to hide her phone while she took photos of the truck's tire prints and some boot prints that were probably Lang's. Back on the county road, she made a little switchback as it climbed the low bluff over the creek. She parked behind some brush, took her massive old Steiner binoculars, and walked until she could see Lang's cabin. She stood out of the sun, behind a little stand of sumac.

She glassed the pickup. A rear window rack held a wooden baseball bat and an old pump .410 shotgun. The cab floor was piled with fast-food litter. In the bed were a few crumpled PBR cans, a rusted weed whip, some spent .410 shells, and a small coil of quarter-inch sisal rope. The coil had been opened and was held together with a knotted strip of cloth. The cut end was slightly frayed.

Bond drove to Alice Lang's house in Wapanucka. There was not yet any crime scene tape on the property. The brown frame house was fenced, on every side but the street, with tall arborvitae trees that had grown together. You couldn't see into or out of any window that was not on the front of the house. She parked on a concrete apron behind the detached garage, took some disposable gloves from a box in the console, and snapped them on.

She opened the fuse box and took Alice Lang's spare house key, which lay on top of some spare fuses. She opened the back door with the key, without touching the knob, and put the key back in the box. She took off her boots outside. When she stepped onto a kitchen throw rug, the room was dark. Bond could see all the way to the front of the house, and all the venetian blinds were dropped and closed. Someone besides Alice had done that, and it had required some time. Alice liked a bright house. Both the kitchen counter and the dining table were clear and clean, and a dish towel, neatly draped over the oven handle, was clipped with a daisy pin. Clipping the dish towel was usually the last thing Alice did before she left the house—right after she had cleaned all surfaces and washed any dirty dishes or utensils that had been used since she came into the house. "Tidy grandma from Dusseldorf," she often said to Hannah as she was clipping the towel.

So if Lang was taken from her house, she was taken as she entered it. Her purse was still on the counter near the back door. It had no zipper. Bond reached inside and spread the wallet's cash slot with her fingernail. It was empty, which these days meant nothing. Three credit cards were nestled in their slots.

The .22 rifle was still behind the kitchen door. Bond tilted her head back and inhaled deeply. She had never smoked, and her nose was keen. Alice Lang's house usually smelled faintly of three things: old natural gas in its plaster walls, dryer sheets, and Pine-Sol. Today there were new scents in the mix: "boy"—that catchall for the sweat of men under thirty—and anise, sage, and oak smoke. An hour ago, Jeff Lang was burning oak. But she reminded herself that his woodpile was whatever deadwood came easiest.

If the intruder had rifled the place, he had, as far as she could see from the kitchen, put everything back in its drawer or cabinet. Bond mentally walked into every room Alice Lang would never see again. She remembered feeling the same thing after her little sister was murdered: that the rooms missed her and needed her. Bond knew that Alice herself was the rooms, but it didn't make sense that way. Her restless straightening hand was everywhere visible in the house. Pressed tablecloth, buffed oak floor, spotless windows and mirrors, bedspread symmetrically draped. The place always looked staged, like a museum house. Bond shook her head. Without Alice, the linens and bowls and chairs would be scattered, the polished surfaces would grow dim.

A backfire up the road brought Bond to the beveled window in the front door. She saw, in the ghostly blur of the framing prism, Jeff Lang's pickup creeping from behind the rank of arborvitae. She took a step back, out of the light, and looked through clear glass. The truck stopped, idled roughly. His bald head, with its red spike of beard, popped out the window. Bond could see his eyes moving over the house, but his face was expressionless. He pulled his head inside the cab, faced ahead, and stomped the accelerator.

CHAPTER 9

There was nothing at the Ada address on Lon Crum's HR file and photocopied driver's license but a chain-wall foundation and the slab and door of a buried tornado shelter. No building debris, no carbon on the concrete—the house had been gone a long time. So the HR address was not a shot in the dark. Maytubby yanked open the shelter door and shined his light down the stairs. Brown water a foot deep, a crutch floating in it.

The house next door had cardboard window panes and Visqueen storm windows, the plastic sheeting fastened to the window frames with thumbtacks. When he knocked on the front door, Maytubby saw that a rolled bath towel had been stuffed under the sweep.

The door opened, and a figure buried by clothing motioned Maytubby in, quickly shut the door, and kicked the towel back under the sweep. The low blue flame of an old radiant heater was the only light in the room and the only heat in the house. "Sorry it's so cold." An elderly woman's voice. "And dark. But airn 'lectric or gas boss linin' his size-forty britches with my dead husband's sweat money. And I don't take no charity."

"No ma'am."

"Now, Mr. Policeman, what is it *you* want out of me? I got airn car, pistol, whiskey, nor hot property."

Maytubby trained his flashlight on the photo of Lon Crum. "This young man, when he was filling out a job application, gave the empty lot next door as the address of his residence."

"He did, did he?"

"Do you recognize him?"

"Do I recognize him? I even know why he done what he done. So when he thieved from work, they couldn't find him."

Maytubby looked at the blue flames reflected in the woman's eyes. "Do you know where he lives?"

A low wheeze rattled up from under the flames, and the floor creaked. Maytubby realized that the woman was laughing. "Across the street," she gargled.

"House with the red awnings?"

"That boy is dumb as a shovel." She nodded. "Yeah. That house. I haven't seen him in a spell, now that *all* my windows are cardboard."

"Did you see him hanging out with anybody in particular? When you still had some glass?"

"He always went off, even when he was real young. You go over there you'll see why."

"No law enforcement officers over there? When you still had glass."

"Oh, yeah. For the mother or father or both. Ragin' drunks."

*   *   *

Before Maytubby knocked on the door shaded by a red awning, he heard the audience of a television game show. After he knocked, a woman inside said, "Well, shit." She snapped the door open. She was holding a sweating plastic OU cup. Maytubby saw at once where Lon Crum got his saggy eyelids and urchin flair.

"Yeah?" she said.

"I'm looking for a young man named Lon Crum."

"Why?" She smiled faintly.

"I'd like to ask him a few questions." Maytubby looked just past her face into the shambles for any sign of the fake guard uniform.

"You can ask *me* a few questions." She leaned against the jamb. Her breath smelled like rotten pears.

"Does Lon Crum live here?"

"Why does a handsome Indian cop want to know?" She kept her eyes on him while she drank from the tumbler.

"Ma'am, I don't know that Mr. Crum has done anything wrong. Could you tell me where I can find him?"

"You want to come in?"

"No thank you, ma'am …"

"Stop with the 'ma'am.' I'm not much older than you are. You think I am because I got a twenty-one-year-old son. You think I have the body of a 'ma'am'?" She looked down at her chest and back to Maytubby.

"Will Mr. Crum be home later this evening? Does he have a work-place, or somewhere he hangs out? A bar?"

"'*Mis*ter Crum.' That's funnier than 'ma'am.' Maybe you didn't notice, but this ain't England, and my son ain't no country gentleman. This is Bumfuck, Oklahoma, and my son is a broke-dick loser just like his daddy, the other *Mis*ter Crum. I kicked 'em both out. Couple months ago. Workplace is one place you won't find either one of 'em." She side-eyed Maytubby and giggled. "Me, either, looks like."

"Do you know where your son is living now?"

She shook her head. "He shows up ever now and then, to get some-thing he forgot. Never has told me where he's staying at. I asked him last time, too." The OU cup went to her lips. She took a long draft.

"Does he ever ask for money?"

"Not since he moved out. You *are* asking me a few questions."

"I appreciate your help."

"Oh, God." She lifted and lowered her hands like a marionette. "Make him a real boy!"

"Have you noticed anything different about him?"

She sighed and looked at the ceiling. "Oh. He's more offish, I guess.

Don't ever look at me. Don't act pissed at me. Kind of like a zombie."

"You notice anything different about his shoes?"

"He didn't start wearing high heels, if that's what you mean."

"No."

She scanned the floor again as if looking at her son's shoes. "Sssssss. Not the same ratty red tennis shoes, last time. Darker. Shiny. Shit, I can't hardly remember that." The coquette had gone out of her.

"Was he wearing gloves?"

"No. He never would do outdoor work where you had to wear gloves. Lord, I hope he ain't in any *real* trouble."

"I hope not, Mrs. Crum."

"Marlene."

"Thank you, Marlene."

"I think I did hear him tell somebody on the phone once to meet him at Tim's Roadhouse, out by Stratford."

"Thank you again."

"Marlene."

"Marlene."

She watched him put on his campaign hat as he walked across her dirt yard.

CHAPTER 10

One minute before his shift began, Maytubby parked his cruiser in front of Chickasaw Lighthorse Police headquarters on the west end of Main in Ada. The building sported a new facade—metal siding overhang and stucco ground floor, in the manner of new rural high schools. The dispatcher/receptionist buzzed Maytubby in. He stopped at her desk. "Hey, Sheila."

"I'm really sorry again about Tommy Hewitt. His little girls?"

"They were asleep."

She nodded slowly. Maytubby was grateful she said nothing. "Chief wants to talk to you."

"Thanks."

He walked on thick old carpet into the dark warren of offices. Chief Les Fox's was the first and the biggest. It also had the biggest interior window. Fox saw everyone who entered and left. He motioned Maytubby in. The nation's governor, in a large framed photo, gazed with amiable impassiveness over the chief's shoulder.

Fox turned from his laptop screen and faced Maytubby. The glass on the governor's portrait reflected Fox's screen. He was playing solitaire, and old Sol was winning. "Sit down, Bill. You had a tough day yesterday. I thought you would be the right person to notify Mrs. Hewitt."

Maytubby nodded.

"How is she?"

"Not good."

Fox shook his head. "Too bad." He looked at his hands a few seconds and then said, "You know I can't assign you to this case. The main reason is jurisdiction. Member of the nation is killed on nation land, no evidence an Indian did it. That's fed business."

"No evidence the killer wasn't an Indian."

"Even if he is, you were too close to Tommy Hewitt."

Maytubby watched Fox's eyes.

"Anything goes wrong, it's chalked up to revenge," Maytubby said. He had intended, after this planned admission, to flank his boss. But Maytubby didn't say anything.

"Correct. I'm glad we understand each other."

The chief's speech was smudged with irony. Maytubby was right about the eyes. A smile ghost in there.

Fox said, "I need you to stay on the trail of those rustlers in Nebo. They are striking fear in the hearts of our fellow citizens down there."

Oh. Okay. Don't flog it.

"That's your only assignment. And I'm hands-off. You are free to move about the nation as your investigation demands."

By now Fox was almost winking at him. Maytubby stood up. "Got it," he said.

The chief swiveled his chair and resumed his administrative duties.

As Maytubby softly closed the door, he looked down the empty hall and said, "Huh."

Though the sun shone brightly outside, the interior of headquarters, wherever there was no fluorescent, was dark as a cave. Maytubby walked slowly toward his office, dreading the metal in-box and the glass in-box. Without the tubes overhead, the only light in his office was a pillbox window that framed a slit of rolling prairie.

Maytubby scooted his laptop aside and opened a worn copy of

Oklahoma Atlas and Gazetteer to the page containing the tiny grid that represented Wilson. One by one, in his memory, he followed the roads leaving Wilson, until his memory ran out, usually at one of the nation's borders. Sometimes, he was looking across the Red River into Texas.

As the houses and barns drifted by, he looked for signs of—not neglect, but inattention. Signs that whoever lived in a house was preoccupied with something bigger than the property. The land surrounding a building might be leased, so ruling out working farms and ranches wouldn't help.

An hour into this exercise, he was almost lost in a back-road reverie sixty miles from Wilson when he realized he hadn't driven that stretch of blacktop for many years and that he had no idea what the houses would look like now.

He slapped the atlas shut, leaned back in his chair, and gazed across the Red. Texas was really big.

CHAPTER 11

Jim's Roadhouse had occupied an abandoned Onan gas station since Maytubby was young. The oil company sign, black letters on gold, had never been painted over. Neither had the smaller sign beneath it, PUMP YOURSELF. Plenty of Stratford's citizens read the Bible and might have seen the funny, but Maytubby suspected that the story of Onan, whom God punished for spilling his seed upon the ground, was not a regular sermon topic.

Jim's was between Ada and Stratford, the Peach Capital of the World—one of seven in the United States. Maytubby parked at the end of a line of middle-aged pickups. Behind Jim's, a peach orchard spread north, its small gnarled trees like frozen scourges. When he opened the metal door, cigarette smoke rolled over him. But the place smelled more of Onan's spilled oil than either booze or smoke. Maytubby recognized the bartender. "Hey, June," he said, quickly to cut the cop tension. The half-dozen silverbacks at the bar resumed talking. He didn't have to look at their faces to know that Lon Crum was not in the room.

"Hey, Bill. Long time, no see."

"Sorry about the café."

"Thanks." She wrinkled her nose. "Ancient history."

"I still miss your peach salsa."

"I know you, buster. You figured out the recipe and make it at home."

"Could be."

"Who you looking for?"

He unfolded a photo and held it out to her. "Lon Crum. Used to live with his mother in Ada."

She took the photo, held it a second under the register's desk lamp, then snapped it back at him. "He comes in every few months. Just long enough in between that I card him and then remember I carded him the time before. I call him Pigpen. Not to his face."

"He meet anybody?"

She looked up the bar, down a row of empty tables. "Good question. I know if he met a girl I would remember that. That's rare in this place. I don't remember, Bill. Sometimes, I get busy. Show it around to these old turds."

Lon Crum's mug shot roused the old turds. They tilted their heads back to get the highest diopter in their trifocals, shifted the picture until it got the most neon light. Almost ten minutes passed before the last man told Maytubby he didn't recognize Crum.

"Gimme your card, Bill. If I remember, I'll call you next time he comes in."

Seventy-five minutes later, in fading light, Maytubby drove past the Golden Play Casino to the first intersection west, Dog Pen Road. Knocking at the house nearest the intersection and working outward, he asked if anyone had seen a white Supercab go by around one in the afternoon the day before. Everybody knew about the robbery and murder. Nobody had been home.

With his strobes on, he drove slowly down the shoulder of US 70, looking through the imaginary eyeholes of the getaway driver's pirate mask. He also looked for discarded pieces of the fake guard uniforms. At Tribble Road, Maytubby stopped. He looked in every direction and saw neither house nor vehicle. Easy place to vanish.

The pirate king had to get off the highway before he ran into sheriff's deputies or the OHP. Driving north took him right into Healdton. May-tubby turned south. At the intersection of Whiskey Lane, he noticed an older man unloading sacks of pig starter from the bed of his pickup into a trailer hitched to an old tractor. The man saw the cruiser pull up his drive but continued to load his sacks. When Maytubby got close to him, he turned and smiled, lifted and reseated his flapped corduroy cap. He had spidery fingers.

"So I call the sheriff, and the Indian police come. Maybe I should of called the Indian police."

"What did you want to tell the sheriff's office?"

"I seen that pickup from the robbery yesterday."

"How did you know it was the same pickup?"

The man pointed north up Tribble Road and traced it back to the intersection. "He came from up there and hardly slowed down when he came 'round left." His finger followed Whiskey Lane eastward. "I thought that truck was going to roll. Another reason I know it was the same truck, KXII said there was men in the back of the pickup. Well, there was men in the back of this pickup."

"Anything else unusual?"

"Yeah."

Maytubby waited. There was a twinkle in the pig-starter man's eyes.

"Must have been really unusual."

"Was."

"The driver was wearing a pirate mask."

The twinkle disappeared, and Maytubby felt a little mean.

"Yeah," the man said, flat.

"You see anybody throw anything out?"

"Happened pretty quick."

"Did you see him turn off Whiskey Lane?"

The pig starter man squinted as he stared down the road. Maytubby's questions reignited the twinkle. "Like Moses said, it turned not from it neither to the right hand nor to the left hand."

On the back of one of his cards, Maytubby wrote the phone number of the US Attorney's Office for Western Oklahoma. He handed it to the rancher. "Officially, the feds are investigating this, not the sheriff. Give them a call and tell them what you told me."

Two miles from the intersection, Whiskey Lane rose over a small hill and vanished from the rancher's view. Reluctant to give up on his vision of the getaway, Maytubby did not stop before Jehovah Road. No one answered the door at any of the three houses nearest the intersection.

Driving north, he saw in the distance a low-slung white metal building that appeared to be flashing, like an electric road-construction sign. Nearing it, he saw the blue star of a welder's arc, and bursts of orange sparks. The welded object—some sort of structural frame—was too big to fit inside the metal building. A listing aqua Bronco pickup from the seventies sat in the lot, two gas cylinders upright in its bed. The building's large sliding doors were open, so the welder was likely working alone. If this was a business, it had no sign.

After the welder had played his electrode to a nub, he lifted his hood with a heavy black glove. When Maytubby made eye contact with him, the welder, in his early thirties, remained seated and said, "Yeah?"

"You heard about the robbery and murder at the Golden Play yesterday?"

"Sure did. *Terrible* thing." The man shook his head dolefully, the hood making him look like a comic stage horse. "Whoever done that had a heart of frozen ice. Widowed a wife and one-half orphaned the children. It's a dern abomination."

"Have you read or seen a description of the getaway vehicle?"

"I have not, Officer."

Maytubby held out a photo of a matching pickup. The welder cradled it ceremoniously in his stiff leather glove. Matted sandy hair framed his gray eyes. As he studied the photo, he rubbed his chin with the other gloved hand like an eighth-grade thespian.

This man was too old to be such a sorry liar, Maytubby thought as he looked past the welder and quickly scanned the metal building. The low winter sun flung some dim amber light through the open garage doors—not enough to be helpful. That building would hold a pickup.

"You know, Officer ..." The welder scrunched his brows. "This picture reminds me. I *did* see a pickup like this yesterday. It was going like a house afire."

"Which direction?" Maytubby already knew what he would say, and noted the absence of floodlights on the property.

"That way," pointing in the direction Maytubby had come.

Maytubby took the photo back and folded it. "Anything unusual about the truck or the driver?"

Again the chin-rubbing. "I believe the driver was wearing a gold baseball cap."

"Gold like Byng High?"

"Whut?"

"That's their color, the Byng Pirates."

Even in the shadow of the hood, Maytubby could see him flinch. The welder looked down and shrugged. "I didn't see nothin' *on* the hat," he said to the ground.

"You've been a big help," Maytubby said. The welder looked up. "Do you know Lon Crum?"

"Long Crumb? What kind of name is that?" The welder looked genuinely at a loss.

"Doesn't matter, man. Thank you very much."

"Sure," the welder said. He clamped a fresh rod and flipped his hood down.

In case the welder was watching, Maytubby drove back the way he came, turning his rearview mirror toward the metal building. Only a few seconds passed before the arc died and the hood went up and pivoted.

If the pirate king did hide his truck and crew in that building until dark yesterday, Maytubby thought, he could have gone either to the right hand (north) or to the left hand (south). But the welder had raised the odds on the right.

CHAPTER 12

When Hannah Bond saw Jeff Lang coming out of the Tille Mart in Wapanucka with a six-pack of Hamm's, she was glad she had decided not to break into his house. He would have caught her. Lang saw the cruiser and shot Bond the finger, moving it up and down slowly.

Back at the bend on State 7, she switched on her radar, woke her laptop, and searched "Alice Lang" on the *Ada News* website. Once she passed the few headlines about Lang's murder, the next results were from a decade before. "Bookkeeper Pleads Guilty to Embezzlement." Bond stared at the headline. *Alice Lang?*

The cruiser radar beeped. She swatted it off.

MUSKOGEE. In Federal District Court, Richard James, from Sulphur, pleaded guilty Thursday to the charge of embezzlement and theft of more than $1000 from an Indian tribal organization. An investigation by the Chickasaw Nation and the FBI yielded evidence that James had embezzled more than $100,000 from Paska Manufacturing, a Chickasaw steel fabrication enterprise in Marietta. As part of a plea deal, James was sentenced to one month in prison and ordered to repay the Chickasaw Nation. James was arrested six months ago after another accounting officer, Alice Lang, discovered that he had created invoices from a false vendor and collected the money himself.

Two years before Bond was commissioned. Four years before she met Alice. Alice never mentioned it. A black-and-white photo of the felon showed a boyish face—light-colored eyes, delicate features, wispy blond hair.

When Maytubby answered her call, the road noise on his end was loud. "Hannah."

"Hey, Bill. Did you know Alice Lang testified in a big Nation embezzlement case ten years ago?"

"No. Neither of us had a badge back then. Never heard of it from anyone else. She tell you that?"

"No. I was just this minute searching her name on the *Ada News* website, and it came up."

"Did the thief do time?"

"A month plus restitution to the nation. Defense blamed a gambling addiction."

"Good counsel. He got off easy. Not murder-material grudge."

"It's been ten years—a long time to wait, but long enough that people forget."

"And that's no help since the internet forgets nothing."

"Do you know if Scrooby has asked your boss about this?"

"Just a sec." Over the road noise, Bond could hear Maytubby talking to Chief Fox on the two-way. She heard the mike go back in its cradle. "Fox says no. He'd never heard of it, either. Nobody else in the office. Want me to tell Scrooby your news?"

Bond gave him a raspberry.

"Obstruction of justice, Deputy."

"All right, you tell Fox what *you're* doing right now."

"He's looking the other way. You believe it?"

"He's too smart to say that to you. Wink, wink?"

"Yeah."

"Hell must've froze over."

"It was Tommy."

"Course it was. I'll let you go turn over some more rocks."

"Turn over enough, maybe …"

"Yeah, I know. Find a scorpion. Bond activated her radar and looked at her watch. She was short-time on her shift, needed some citations outside the earlier clump … 45, 52, 49, 56, 55, 57 … The parade of law-abiding citizens grew longer. A red-tailed hawk circled high in the golden sunlight … 54, 56, 56, 55 … When she looked up again, the hawk was much lower. It descended gently, then bolted to the ground. It thrashed the roadside grass as it rose heavily, a cottontail in its talons.

Suddenly, the hawk burst in a spume of feathers, and the carcass of the rabbit smacked the cruiser's windshield. Bond was not a flincher, but the rabbit made her blink. She stared at the spattered blood and zigzag crack for less than a second before the flashing radar caught her eye: 112.

As the cruiser stormed onto the pavement, Bond had to look below the rabbit to see the road ahead. The wipers wouldn't budge it. She leaned most of her long torso out the window, grabbed the rabbit's hind legs, and flung it into the ditch. There was no washer fluid, so she threw half a paper cup of black coffee onto the glass, opening a clear streak in the gore, and pulled down the visor to cut the setting sun.

Though the speeder had a quarter-mile lead, Bond knew that it wasn't Jeff Lang, whose clown car would have spilled its drive train long ago. She radioed her dispatcher in Tish and put the Charger through its paces. Holding at 120, she gained on the speeder. Pursuit left her cold unless she had a stake in the chase, which she didn't—yet. As black stands of hackberry trees shot past her window, she reached into a bag of Fritos and tossed a handful into her mouth. They reminded her of Bill Maytubby's strange eating habits. He told her once that he didn't eat "processed foods." That tickled her. "Hell, Bill. What can you eat that's *not* processed—persimmons and raw turnips?" He said something about frozen pizza and fish sticks, but she knew good and well he ate raw turnips. She had seen them on the seat of his cruiser.

Near the Bromide turnoff, the speeder decelerated. Bond was about a hundred yards behind the silver SUV. She thought it was going to turn into the little hills, but it pulled onto the shoulder, hazards flashing. Bond shrugged to herself, radioed Tish that she had stopped a silver 2013 Volvo XC60 SUV, picked up her clipboard, and stepped into the cold prairie wind.

While the passenger window was descending, Bond looked at the trails of blood blown all the way to the back of the roof. She took the license and registration from a stocky man in late middle age, his thinning hair just turning gray. He wore a dark blue suit and stylish glasses.

"I didn't see you until just now," he said, tilting his head to see her face, way above the SUV.

Bond was silent. The license said "Frank Sulak," Cache address. She copied what she had to copy, very slowly, though her hands were cold. In the cruiser, she ran his license. Two minor citations over a decade. Fifty-seven over—what she was citing him for now—stuck out.

While Sulak was taking his citation and paperwork, Bond brought her face closer. "You can do a year for killing a bald eagle."

Sulak instantly wiped a creeping smirk off his face. Bond saw this—when he realized this rube hulk could cuff him, bald eagle or not.

"That was a bald eagle? That's too bad. Noble birds. I would never inten—"

"Rabbit he had—broke my windshield." Bond turned her back on him and walked back to her cruiser.

"I would be happy to pay for the damage," he shouted, his body twisted half around.

Bond slammed her door, pulled onto the highway, and accelerated slowly toward Tishomingo.

CHAPTER 13

Maytubby drove north on Jehovah Road. The ancient Arbuckle Mountains were russet bison humps on the horizon. He was looking for a propane jockey. These guys got around, especially in a cold winter like this one. They worked outside, close to roads. And they were bored, so they noticed what passed by.

Where Jehovah struck State 53 near Milo, Maytubby spotted a Sooner Propane truck next to a leaning hall-and-parlor. When he pulled into the drive, he saw that the guy filling the silver tank was a young woman, her long hair swirling around her earmuffs. She was already staring curiously at the truck photo while he walked toward her. The name stitched on her coveralls was Sarah.

Yes, she had heard about the robbery and murder. "Makes you sick. That man had little children." She shook her head slowly as she watched the pressure gauge.

Maytubby held the photo out to her. "Yesterday? Today?"

"I see that kind of truck, same color, a lot out here. But. This morning." She lowered her head and looked at him conspiratorially. "Just before the sun came up, I saw one on Fifty-Three between

Springer and Gene Autry." She nodded east. "Maybe because I saw the security pictures on my computer before I left for work, it caught my attention. I was filling a tank when this truck came by, kind of slow. One guy driving; all the other seats and the back're empty. The truck turns up a long driveway that goes to a trailer house, and this guy, medium height, pops out of the back, jumps down, and goes into the house. It was too damn cold, that double cab was empty, and that guy didn't look like a Mexican."

"Driveway?"

"Last before the railroad tracks and the Ardmore airport entrance, north side. White-and-gray trailer house, like most. Clothesline, little red pickup. Don't know what kind. That old, they all look alike to me.

"Left the non-Mexican there?"

She nodded. "Then headed toward the Washita."

"You notice if the guy who got out was wearing a uniform?"

"I read about that. Didn't look like it."

"Anybody throw anything out of the truck?"

"Like a pirate mask?"

"That would be helpful."

"No," she said with a faint smile.

"Anything stand out about the driver?"

"Husky. No beard. That's about all I could tell."

"A fat pirate."

"There's lots of fat pirates."

"Yeah?"

"Sure."

Maytubby handed her his card. "In case you see one."

While he was a few miles from the Ardmore airport, Hannah Bond called to tell him about the embezzlement case in Marietta. After he put his phone away, he spotted the trailer, which came with all the right accessories: a red 1980 Chevy LUV in the drive, two pipe clothesline poles in the backyard, a woodpile, and a metal chimney. The woodpile was neatly stacked oak.

Nobody answered his knock. Through the only window without

its white miniblinds closed, he saw two pairs of clean insulated coveralls folded on a chair, an unstained straw Western hat for summer. Medium-size outdoor laborer. No trace of the guard uniform or black gloves or sneakers. There were no dirty dishes in the sink, only clean ones in a drainer. Next to an avocado telephone lay a clean notepad and a sharpened pencil. The kitchen counter and appliances were squeaky clean. There were no ashes in front of the small square woodstove.

An amber gleam caught his eye. The late sun lit a half-full bottle of Blanton's Single Barrel Bourbon, faceted like a gem, with the little metal jockey and horse atop the cork. Maytubby remembered Tommy Hewitt's girls singing along with the television: "*One of these things is not like the others ...*" Whoever bought the whiskey felt big about sharing, thought the poor working stiff would appreciate a taste of the high life. Looking back to the dish drainer, he spotted one highball glass. On the counter, beside a microwave, a plastic liter of Old Cornwipe. So the hooch patron knew what to upgrade.

Maytubby walked across the yard and looked into the fifty-five-gallon drum where the trash was burned. Cold ashes, a few sooty food cans. The little red pickup wore a thick layer of dust, even the windshield. No one had driven it for years. Behind the mobile home, he found the waffle-tread prints of an off-road or dual-sport motorcycle. Dual-sport was street legal.

Maytubby found a little patch of blackjack oaks along the BNSF tracks to screen the cruiser. He looked out over stadium-size freight warehouses that faced Ardmore Municipal's runway. A cargo jet swung onto final approach.

Jill would be home from work. Maytubby called her. "You're still in the field," she said. "Unless the City of Ada built an international airport last night."

"No pulling the wool over your eyes."

"Really, where are you?"

"Ardmore Municipal."

"Oh, yeah. That weird hubbub in the middle of nowhere, like Los Alamos or Las Vegas. You on a stakeout?"

"No. I'm parked behind some trees, waiting for a suspicious person to return home from work so I can observe his movements."

"So, how is that not a stakeout?"

"I'm trying to free my profession from the fetters of machismo."

"You can probably strike off the leg irons without ditching the cool words."

"I think you've naturalized these gendered words."

"I think you're full of shit as a Christmas turkey. You can't go with me to see Nichole tonight. That's why you're calling, right?"

"Yes."

"Okay. I'll tell her you're on a stakeout."

"Give my love to her and the girls. See you tomorrow."

Coming from the east, the yellow cycle crossed the tracks at 5:21. So the guy's job was ten, fifteen miles into the rock prairie, maybe at a dolomite quarry. Maytubby gave the motorcyclist time to get away from his bike and into the house. Then he parked on the highway and walked softly up the drive, on the grass beside the gravel. It was near dark.

Before he knocked, he watched the cyclist, still wearing coveralls and thick gloves, pick the Bourbon up in his right hand, hold it up to the naked kitchen bulb. Then he slid it down the counter and poured two fingers of his cheap whiskey into the tumbler. He bit the right glove's index finger, tugged the glove off. He was early thirties, wispy but trimmed soul patch. His ash-blond hair had recently been cut. His socks matched, and his nails were trimmed. Despite the booze, he had no gut.

Too short to be the meticulous robber, too well-groomed to be the slob, too tall and right-handed to be the shooter. Did the pirate king keep a pit crew? A scout? There were no visible personal electronics. Maytubby watched him take off the other glove and zip out of his coveralls, which he folded and carried down the hall. He came back, turned on a small television, and fell back into a tattered recliner, holding his whiskey out in front so it wouldn't spill on him.

If this was one of the pirate band and Maytubby flushed him, the

man wouldn't lead him to the others. The bike's license plate reflected enough inside light for Maytubby to memorize the numbers.

It was full dark when Maytubby got back in his cruiser. He ran the plate—Francis Klaus, address in Bray, home of the Fighting Donkeys. Then he crossed the Washita on his way to Ada.

At a Chickasaw Travel Stop, he bought a banana and an apple and stretched against the cruiser's fender while he listened to Jill's cell go to voice mail. Banjo lesson night, he remembered. Or she might have gone to Nichole's. He texted that he would see her the next night. In an hour, he was standing on the porch of his old gable-and-wing house, a relic of Indian Territory. It overlooked a Katy railroad cut that had been converted to a bike path. A single naked bulb swung above him in the wind, the shadow of his arm and keys tracing the slab like a pendulum.

It was cold inside. The single ceiling bulb in each room dimly lit panel curtains that trembled in window drafts. A purple metal tumbler half full of water sat on his kitchen table, beside it a dog-eared paperback of *The Selected Poems of Emily Dickinson*. From the refrigerator, he took a small paper bag of nut meats from the native pecan tree that shaded his house. He laid the bag on the table and walked into his bedroom, unzipping his uniform coat as he went. He turned on the radio by his bed and listened to NPR news on Chickasaw-supported KGOU-Ada. He hung his uniform neatly in the closet, then donned his country civvies: a checkered flannel shirt, jeans, and a denim jacket. Work boots, he couldn't do. The New Balance runners blew the whistle on the whole outfit, but he wore them anyway.

Back in the kitchen, he filled a half-gallon milk jug with water; put the pecans in his pocket; grabbed an insulated camo hat, a set of stained Billy Bob teeth, and some old gloves; and turned out the kitchen light. In the yard, he pulled off his cap and mussed his hair. The bully V-8 in his '65 Ford pickup roared to life, its torque jostling the cab.

On the dark empty back roads, he made good time to Jehovah Road. The nearest house to the welder's shop was a quarter mile. Flickers through its closed miniblinds told him the folks were watching television. A locked single-pipe gate blocked the shop's driveway, but a

little trail across the unfenced land next door led Maytubby into a knot of scrub oak. He pocketed his Maglite and set off through the scrub toward the rear of the shop. Coyotes whooped in the low hills. The moon revealed no back entrance, but Maytubby tried each overlap of corrugated metal sheets until he found a patch of rust around some rivets and peeled the sheet back just far enough to squeeze inside.

He snapped on his flashlight and swept the room. A trailered engine-driven welder was parked on the dirt floor. A hand truck held some gas cylinders and a cutting kit. A functional steel workbench was littered with gloves and metal scraps, a hood, some dirty welder's caps. The dirt floor bore a confusion of foot and tire prints. Near the front of the shop, his light found a dented fifty-gallon barrel. It stank of burned plastic. The welder would not have burned trash inside, and indeed, the barrel had dug a wide path where it was dragged in. Maytubby found a length of rebar and stirred the ashes.

When he raised the corrugated rebar, a short black snake was draped over it. He kept his light inside the barrel as he lowered his face. Then he spat on the snake, and soot melted off its brass scales. A zipper.

A vehicle on Jehovah Road slowed and then turned into the welder's drive. Maytubby dropped the zipper into the barrel, then put the rebar back where it belonged. He switched off his Maglite. The vehicle's headlights shot through gaps in the shop's wall. Mussing the floor dirt as he backtracked, Maytubby pushed back the metal flap, eased outside, and lay on the ground. He heard the gate chain clinking, the vehicle moving forward, then the sliding-door chain rattling.

Maytubby peered into the shop. The headlights went dark. He hissed softly into the grass. When the door creaked open, nothing but moonlight lit the frame. A male figure, medium height and build, with a stocking cap and gloves, moved from an older pickup (not a stubby Bronco) to the barrel. The man grasped its lip like a steering wheel, tilted the barrel toward him, and rolled it on its bottom rim, hand-over-hand, toward the pickup bed.

When the loading noise began, Maytubby sprinted for the Ford. He heard the lock chains and the other pickup's engine as he ran. When he spun onto Jehovah Road, he was a half mile behind the northbound pickup. He did not turn on the Ford's headlights but, like Jill Milton, navigated by the moon's luster. Maytubby knew that if he didn't spoil the tail, the investigation was a search warrant ahead.

The pickup did not stop for any crossing roads. Its driver turned off the headlights briefly as he approached them, so he could see lights from another vehicle nearing the crossroads. On the Caddo Creek bridge, the pickup stopped. Maytubby was still far enough in the rear he didn't have to brake and spill red light on the prairie. He switched off the ignition and coasted to a stop while the driver swung up into the bed, lifted the barrel, and banged it on the bridge guardrail to dislodge the ashes.

The creek was small and sluggish. The guy would dump most of the ashes on sand, and if he hit water, the zippers would sink. The pickup's lights came back on, and it sped north. After it found State 53 and headed east, Maytubby was forced to turn on his headlights.

For a while, the two pickups retraced Maytubby's earlier route, past the trailer, through Gene Autry, over the Washita. Then the barrel pickup turned onto a dirt road Maytubby recognized as Powell. It wound up through rocky badlands favored by deer hunters and strip miners. It branched into smaller roads and trails that wound among mining pits and spoil banks—land that had been worked over. He drove past Powell, then, just over a rise, turned off his lights, made a U-turn, and fell in a half mile or so behind the barrel truck.

This moonlight tail was much harder. The road and the rocky landscape it threaded looked a lot alike, and the road twisted so often, Maytubby lost sight of the barrel truck. The old Ford jolted over some large rocks and shuddered over washboard. The moonlit spines of moving deer caught his eye, and he stopped to let them cross the road.

After a few winding miles, he topped a ridge overlooking smaller hills and spoil banks. The ice-haloed moon turned the white rocks blue. Ahead, taillights emerged from behind a hill. They quickly flashed as brake lights, and the truck made a right off Powell. Maytubby waited sixty seconds and followed. He knew the intersection, had always assumed the trail was a driveway. Most of the drives were long, so nobody would hear him drive by on Powell and make his way by back roads to Mill Creek.

Approaching the drive, he cranked down the driver's window so he could listen and looked out the passenger window for any light that might show through the scrubby cedars. An owl cooed down in the wash.

He was thirty yards from the intersection when headlights blazed across Powell Road and then pivoted toward him. He slammed on his brakes as a pickup made directly for him. It stopped two feet from his bumper, and its driver sprang from the cab. Maytubby snapped on his hat and set his gag teeth before the driver appeared at his window, breathing heavily. He was short and stout, and his breath stank of drink.

"The fuck you driving out here 'thout no *lights*? He squeezed a holster Maytubby could barely see but didn't draw the pistol.

Maytubby turned to face the man and waited a beat. "I'm guessin' you're not the game warden."

"The *fuck* you talkin' about?"

"See if I can put a little meat on the table. Growin' kids is hungry."

"Where's your gun at?"

Maytubby rolled his eyes up at the cab's ceiling gun mount, visible in the reflected headlights.

The stubby man bent his knees, turned his head, and squinted up suspiciously. "That's a *shotgun*."

"Uh-huh."

"What kinda retard hunts deer with a shotgun?"

Maytubby shrugged. "My kind, I guess."

The short man breathed heavily.

"Naw. I use slugs in place of buckshot."

"Slugs. That's some hillbilly shit."

"Works. Sometimes. I don't go on people's land. I shoot 'em in the road."

"Bucks, you mean."

"And does."

"But not people."

"What?" Maytubby said.

The man lowered his head and shook it. Then he looked up and said, "You stay the fuck away from here. Way away." He waved an arm at the moon. "You'll kill one of my b … my cattle in the dark like this."

"Oh, I turn on my headlights just before I fire."

"Shit." The man put two fingers to his forehead.

"In the light, I can tell a deer from a cow ever time."

The man turned from the Ford and walked slowly toward his pickup.

"Unless the cow's real poor!" Maytubby called after him.

The man climbed into his cab, slammed the door, and spun gravel in reverse. He was driving a ten-year-old Dodge Dakota, blue, and he got out again to lock a heavy galvanized gate behind him.

A mile down the road, in an uninhabited stretch of open prairie, Maytubby stopped, pulled the twenty-gauge pump from its rack, put a single birdshot shell in the chamber, and fired it into the air. Ease the short man's mind.

He ejected the spent shell, picked it up off the gravel, and put it in his jacket pocket. He stared up at the gambrels of the sky. Orion was very blue, except for Betelgeuse, that vast dying sun, which was orange. As he was stowing the shotgun, his cell buzzed. A 580 area code, local. "Maytubby," he said.

"Bill, it's June, at the Road House."

"You calling to report a slob?"

"You didn't have to wait long."

"Quickest I can get there is forty-five minutes." He switched on his headlights and pushed the Ford along the rocky straightaway. "He alone?"

"No. With a husky middle-aged man dressed nice."

"Sticks out among the old turds."

"Like a rooster on a mud fence."

"Can you send me a picture of them in case they leave before I get there?"

"I got a crappy phone. You'll get what you pay for."

"Thanks, June."

A quarter hour later, Maytubby was driving past the Hewitts' house. Nichole's mother's car was parked behind hers, and the house was dark. A sodium lamp threw amber light on the yard and house. His eyes got hot, and he felt a little queasy. He drove too fast getting to the highway in Mill Creek and then too fast leaving Mill Creek behind. Nichole and her little girls couldn't drive away from themselves.

Onan might have been cursed by God, but his parking lot was full. Tim's was doing a land-office business. Maytubby parked his old Ford at the edge of the concrete, donned his cap, and put in his Billy Bob teeth. As he walked, he looked at the old turds' pickups. Ten-year-old Chevy, ten-year-old Ford, Crum's 1991 Ford, fifteen-year-old Ford, ten-year-old Dodge, new Volvo SUV. Whup. Rooster on a mud fence. Maytubby thought of the Blanton's bottle. He memorized the plate—didn't call it in to headquarters, because he didn't want to be caught loitering among men's trucks in the dark.

When he walked into the bar, he smiled at June. She frowned and nodded—didn't recognize him. Crum and the dude sat at a Formica table in a dark corner of the bar. Reflected neon gave Crum's fish-belly moonface a spectral violet glow. Maytubby thought he looked like the ghost of Pap Finn Future. Of the dude, he could see only a bald patch and a blazer collar that had seen a tailor.

There were no empty tables. He stood at the far end of the bar and ordered a Bud Light, walked to the juke box, just behind Crum, and knitted his brow with deliberation. The loud whiny country tune rode its final tonic chord to an abrupt stop. The sudden silence caught the dude off guard. His loud last word was "Choc-a-Bubbies." The "Bubbies" part came out softer.

Up and down the song menu—a wasteland of country songs. Choc-a-Bubbies? Strange-sounding fodder for criminal intrigue. But pretty damned specific, whatever they were. Crum and the dude talked softly. Maytubby put his mind into his peripheral vision and blocked out the song titles he was staring at. The dude rolled his eyes now and then, once when he said "fucking eagle" a little louder than the words around it. He then frowned and jabbed a finger at Crum, who was smoking. The finger bristled with black hair. Maytubby could see the back of Crum's head. And wished he couldn't. "… them all," the dude said. "I can do that," Crum said. Then Maytubby saw the dude look up at the jukebox. One random hymn to self-pity coming up.

When he got to the register, Maytubby turned his back to the room, looked at June, and took out his goober teeth. She squinted at him. "You."

"Thanks for the heads-up, June."

"I sent you a picture of 'em anyway. You look scroungy in that getup. And those teeth—you scared me."

"So the eye patch would have been too much."

"I would have called you and told you to hurry up."

"Odd pair, huh?"

"That older guy really sticks out when he comes in here. Which is hardly ever."

"He ever come in alone?"

"No. He meets Pigpen."

"They ever argue?'

She shook her head.

"Ever see them exchange anything?"

She tapped a pencil eraser against her teeth and gazed into the past. "No. But I haven't spied on them. Until tonight."

"Who pays?"

"Soon as you leave, these old turds are going to ask me who you are. Slicker pays. Doesn't tip, either."

"Tell them I'm the beer inspector."

"Fffffff."

While he sat in his cold pickup watching moonlight on peach trees, Maytubby weighed which vehicle to tail. The address on Crum's registration was his mother's, so where he lived remained a mystery. Probably nearby, whereas the dude might lead him far afield.

When the tavern's door swung open and music spilled into the dark orchards, Crum and the dude said no farewells but walked away from each other, toward their vehicles. Watching the lumbering Crum, Maytubby decided to follow the Volvo. Crum drove away while the dude sat in his SUV and talked on his cell a few minutes, the blue glow of the phone illuminating a crescent of his head.

The dude took it slow through downtown Stratford, but as soon as the city limits sign was behind him, he ate up the prairie. Maytubby had to give him a half mile because the highway was deserted. The Ford's big eight didn't complain at a hundred, but the front end floated—took a little too long to obey the steering wheel. He was used to that lag when he was in a cockpit, but it bothered him on the ground. Scanning the road for deer was pointless—he was overdriving his headlights by a thousand feet.

They went straight south to Sulphur, where there was some traffic around the Artesian Hotel, a replica of the big territorial hotel built to lodge pilgrims to the town's magical stinking waters. The replica housed a casino and was rumored to lure Texans. Maytubby moved much closer to the Volvo. At the only stoplight, he could see the dude, in front of him, holding a phone to his ear and running his hand over his head. When the light turned, Maytubby gave the Volvo a long lead before he followed it into the Chickasaw National Recreational Area. They wound slowly through the decommissioned national park, between WPA stone shelters, over WPA stone bridges, past rangers. At the park boundary, marked by bison fencing, the Volvo's exhaust blew sand off the asphalt. The dude quickly hit a hundred.

The terrain grew hillier, and the Volvo, a half mile ahead of Maytubby, disappeared and reappeared. Sometimes he saw the blue cell glow in the SUV, sometimes not.

Ten miles south of Sulphur, Maytubby topped a hill, felt his body lift against the seatbelt. Just over the crest, the Volvo's taillights appeared, not fifty yards ahead of him. He jammed the Ford's brakes, gripped the wheel to check the old truck's rightward slew. The taillights came too fast, and he was forced to pass. He honked long, as if he were angry. The Volvo could not have been doing more than forty.

Maytubby had no choice but to keep the speedometer's quaint red needle pushed against the 100 pin. The dude would soon speed up, but Maytubby's cover was blown.

What had the stubby man stopped himself from saying? "My *boss'* cattle"? Maytubby didn't know every rancher in the Chickasaw Nation, but a new Volvo SUV would have made its owner conspicuous. Maybe. The Powell Road intersection appeared in the moonlight. Maytubby reprised his earlier U-turn, parked behind a red cedar, and turned off his lights. In less than thirty seconds, a pair of headlights approached, slowed, and pivoted into Powell Road.

"Well, well," he said.

He waited, then followed, as he had before, by moonlight alone. Orion had traversed half the sky.

When the Volvo neared the galvanized gate, Maytubby stopped on a rise, turned off his truck, and rolled down the driver's window. The stubby man's truck was parked across the drive, where the gate usually was. When the Volvo approached, the truck backed off the drive to let it pass. Then the stubby man got out and shut the gate. Maytubby heard no dogs, just gravel popping under tires. Two sets of taillights wandered up and over a rise, disappeared.

Parking off the road, on the rise, Maytubby got out. In white spray paint, KEEP arched over the top of an old tire; OUT smiled from the bottom. The tire hung on a fencepost. In the moonlight, the words seemed to float in the air. Maytubby pushed down the lowest strand of barbed wire and swiveled through the fence. No climbing. His father had been rough with him on the subject of fences. Climbing strained the staples and posts. Making fence was hard work, not to be undone by fools.

Following the fence-line cow path to dodge prickly pears and rocks, he watched for a branch off that would lead to water or a feed trough. He walked softly and fast. He had almost reached the driveway when a new path opened to his right. It took the course of least resistance around the base of the hill that the driveway climbed straight up. Then it joined the driveway (separated from it by a fence) and paralleled it for a half mile or so, disappearing into a shining lattice of leafless trees. Beyond the grove, he could make out the bobbing horse head of an oil pumpjack.

Maytubby began to run. He soon relaxed into his stride, and the fumes of Onan were dispelled by winter night air, which smelled faintly of chlorine and straw. Miles to the west a BNSF freight blew for the Redwing crossing before it settled alongside the Washita rapids in Big Canyon.

He went under the lattice and lost the moonlight, slackened his pace. Another half mile, then a cluster of buildings appeared in the middle distance, all of them beneath the winter canopy—a sprawling blond-brick ranch style, a double-wide manufactured home, a large metal building, and a long, narrow metal shed that garaged a half-dozen trucks. He didn't think he saw the Volvo, but it was pretty dark, and he was a long way off. There were no sodium lamps, only the pale glow of shaded light in a few windows.

The cow path angled off to the right before it came up against fence and headed away from the compound. Before Maytubby could stoop to push down a strand of barbed wire, a match flared against the blond brick. It jitterbugged and went out. The orange cigarette tip was dimmer, but Maytubby could follow it and see the shadowy form of its owner, who did not stand in one place like someone going outside just to smoke. The smoker walked around the house, then around the garage, then around the other buildings. He didn't stop, either. Maytubby would need a warrant to get any closer.

When the smoker walked behind the garage, Maytubby walked slowly back down the cow path until he was out of sight of the buildings. Then he ran again, listening to coyotes yodeling in the wash.

*　*　*

A little metallic light in the east. Maytubby was parked in the Ardmore Municipal Airport public lot, waiting for the man in the gray-and-white mobile home to leave for work on his bike. A BNSF freight hauling titanic blades for wind turbines blew for the Highway 53 grade crossing across from the parking lot. Maytubby ate a handful of pecans and drank cold water. He awakened his phone and found a text from Jill Milton: "If any harm comes to this man, you will be sorry you were ever born."

He typed, "To late ladie."

Maytubby was looking at his phone screen when he heard the bike rev up between train horns. When the train had passed, the biker threaded the crossing gates before they lifted, and was almost to the Washita bridge before Maytubby got out of the parking lot. A few minutes later, Maytubby was close enough to see the bike turn onto Powell Road. The plume of dust in gathering light made the tail easy. When the biker passed the compound, Maytubby was relieved. Beyond Oil Creek, they broached a little galaxy of strip mines. The biker slowed and rattled over a cattle guard at the entrance to the X-Silica glass sand mine. Steady day job.

Maytubby's house was cold. He laid his camo hat and Billy Bob teeth on the kitchen table but still wore his jeans jacket and running shoes when he fell into bed.

CHAPTER 14

Hannah Bond waited impatiently until the decent hour of 8 a.m. to ring the doorbell of Cathy Barker, retired Supreme Court justice for the Chickasaw Nation. The judge volunteered at the food pantry with Bond and Alice Lang. If anyone remembered the James embezzlement, Barker would. Bond didn't know when she had fallen asleep. Her laptop was tented on the floor beside the couch, its cord draped over her neck. She had spent most of the night in a fruitless search for details in the James case. She did learn that in the United States there were more than two thousand people named Richard James.

The retired justice poured coffee into old Frankoma Pottery mugs. A Paul Walsh acrylic still life with persimmons hung next to a rack of aprons. Barker stood at her kitchen bar; Hannah Bond sat. That made them the same height.

"Poor Alice," Barker said. "In courtrooms, I've listened to many a ghastly tale in this country, but what happened to her. Her last hour. I can't think about it. And you have to."

"Technically, I don't. Sheriff Magaw turned the investigation over to OSBI."

"Well," Barker said, looking down at her coffee. Then, looking at Bond, "OSBI has a spectrometer. It also has a time clock."

Bond slid a printout of the *Ada News* story across the bar. Barker plucked reading glasses from her short gray hair and slid them up the bridge of her nose. Four seconds later, she pushed the article back and removed her glasses. "You and I never talked about that. You and Alice?"

Bond shook her head.

"Alice was not easily disturbed. But that case—the investigation, the arrest and trial—it rattled her. She had trained that boy. And he did seem like a boy—cherubic, naive, impulsive, eager to please."

"What's 'cherubic'?"

"Like a baby angel. As time went by, Alice began to take a maternal interest in him. Brought him food, nursed him when he was ill, helped him with practical things. He didn't ever speak of a family. She convinced her boss to give him more responsibility."

"Mmmm," Bond growled.

"I know you're thinking about that disturbed nephew."

Bond looked out the window and nodded.

"Yes. The first time she found a crumpled envelope in the angelic boy's trash from a vendor she didn't recognize, she wrote down the address—a post office box in Wichita Falls. There was no such company in that town. Purchasing had never heard of it. She told me she was sure it was some sort of rogue phishing expedition by an outsider. But the same day, Friday, after work, she followed him past his apartment in Marietta, down I-35, across the Red—"

"That must've cost her. Long honking bridge."

Barker tilted her head and narrowed her eyes. "You know what, Hannah? She told me she was so upset she didn't even notice the bridge." Barker sipped her coffee. "An hour later, James walked down the steps of the downtown post office in Wichita Falls, carrying a single legal envelope. He drove to Green National Bank in Ardmore, made an after-hours deposit, and went back to his apartment. Alice told her boss, who called the US Attorney's Office in Muskogee. The investigation didn't take long, but Alice lost a lot of sleep. She told me she felt guilty, knew that was irrational. After his plea deal, James never showed his face again. But his court-ordered restitution payments always arrived on time.

"When he was stealing, did anyone see him spending it?"

"No. And where all that money went remains unclear. He made large withdrawals and claimed to have a gambling addiction. I've never heard of anyone seeing him at a casino. His defense attorney—who was not, by the way, a PD—produced some receipts from the Golden Play. Nobody in security there or at any other casino stepped forward. Once the feds had compiled enough evidence to convict James, I don't think they cared how he spent it." Barker crooked-smiled. "That isn't to say they were happy about the sentence."

"Did Alice care how he spent it?"

"She hates gambling, period—something about a fallen cousin— but she did her best not to think about him."

"Do you know what bank the restitution checks were drawn on?"

"I saw it. The first check passed through my office. Let's see. Generic bank name. In Tulsa." She studied the fine acrylic still life with persimmons on her kitchen wall.

"You don't forget much. Maybe James picked that bank because it has a name that disappears."

"Why would he do that?"

"Did Alice think he was smart?"

"She never made a point of it. He did leave that crumpled envelope from the false vendor lying around."

"Maybe somebody else picked the bank."

Barker frowned and looked at her friend.

"Do you ever run the alphabet when you're trying to remember something?"

"Oh, yes. Shoot. It's the first three letters, Hannah. American Bank of Commerce."

Bond wrote the bank's name very carefully in the margin of the printout and added "Tulsa."

"So, you are suggesting that James *conspired* to embezzle?"

"I don't know." She shrugged. "After the plea, no business is ever letting that kid get anywhere near its books. What other kind of job could a felon get? And even if somebody gave him a decent job, these peckerwood thieves are never real particular about deadlines."

"Wichita Falls—not a taxing drive from Marietta. And across the state line. A border is just a legal fiction, but it throws up mental ramparts. Texas is not here, but there. A fake vendor in Oklahoma would set off alarms when one in Texas might not. Like, 'No wonder I don't know that vendor. It's in Texas.'"

"James went there by his lonesome to get the check and banked it just far enough from home nobody would pay him any mind. So if there's some big crook back of him, that guy's not in Wichita Falls."

"Tulsa—well. We're back to mind-forged boundaries. Marietta could be said to lie in Oklahoma City's orbit. Art-deco old-oil Tulsa commands the Arkansas. It has a different area code."

"Yeah," Bond said, "James might just as well have been in St. Louis. But he wasn't—or isn't. That's another reason I think somebody's pulling his wars."

For half a second, Barker frowned at "wars" before she translated it to "wires," nodded and said, "From a place between Wichita Falls and Tulsa."

"I hope so." Hannah carried her mug to the kitchen sink and rinsed it out. "And even that's a considerable patch of ground—most of it over the Johnston County line."

CHAPTER 15

"Nichole was asleep when I went over there. It wasn't even seven o'clock. Her mother told me she had slept almost around the clock. The girls had just fallen asleep in their mom's bed." Jill Milton stood in the empty, unlit gym of the nation's Ada wellness center. The gym was a foyer to her office in the back. A small sign behind her read, "Jill Milton, PhD." Beneath that, "Nutritionist" and an arrow. She had not included the degree when she ordered the sign. Anemic winter light from the center's bank of windows pooled behind her. "Nichole did ask her mother if there was any news."

"I haven't talked to Fox about what the FBI knows," Maytubby said. "On my end, just a little this side of wild surmise. I think I've found a person who hid the robbers' truck and burned the fake casino guard uniforms they wore."

"An accomplice."

"That, too."

"The feds could question him, but that would alert the confederacy."

"Yeah. And speaking of, a couple of suspicious persons I tailed in my truck through the inky wilds of Johnston County ended up at the same gate. Which had a guard. Who stopped me while I was on a county road."

"How did that go?"

"I deceived him with the camo hat and gag teeth, claimed I was pot-shooting deer."

"You wore your city-man running shoes, didn't you?"

"Well, it was dark."

"Yeah."

"And before that, I had to run really fast."

"Sure. Did you sleep?"

"This morning."

"Doesn't look like it."

"I did run really fast. What do you know about Choc-a-Bubbies?"

"What?

"Like, what are they? Where do they live?"

"They're chocolate-and-caramel candy bars. One by itself is a Bubby. Off-brand, made in Tulsa. The only place they live I care about is school vending machines. Sell like hotcakes, judging by the real estate they're occupying in the machines—lately, especially."

"In your crosshairs."

"Most of the parents and administrators would prefer healthier choices. Soon, the feds will demand it. But the machines bring cash to poor schools, and junk food sells. Strange you should ask, though. The school districts where we put on the Eagle play have been talking about food choices. I've been to some of the meetings. Lately, this guy from Sentinel Vending in Ardmore has been showing up, raising a stink when anybody questions his product."

"Free country, free enterprise, gummint meddling."

"Yeah, the party line, but more personal."

"Small company, a lot at stake?"

"No, not defensive or scared. He's an alpha."

"You're saying people are afraid of him?"

Jill nodded slightly. "He's kind of roosterish, with tiny cold eyes. Menacing eyes."

"You think he owns the company?"

"He doesn't strike me as someone who would inspire loyalty in his employees."

"Did you look for him on the company's website?"

"No photos of people on the website."

"He doesn't load the machines."

"I've seen only two of those people: a man and a woman, and he's not the man. I almost wish he were. At least, he's clean. I wouldn't touch anything I knew that service guy had handled."

"The service guy—what's he look like? Besides the crust."

"Pale. Greasy hair sticking out from under his stocking hat. Stringy beard. Needs suspenders."

"Did you notice if his socks matched?"

"No, but if they didn't, that would be the least of his problems."

"I think this guy's name is Lon Crum. The chief of security at Golden Play thought he might have recognized him on the security video, as one of the impostor guards in the robbery. Crum had been fired from the travel stop next door for shoplifting."

"Somebody must be hard up for gang members. Can't see him doing the runaway part."

"If he's the guy on the tape, you wouldn't. He lumbers. Just didn't have far to go. His body-flop into a pickup bed ..."

"Now, that I can see."

"Last night, I tried to eavesdrop on Crum and an older, richer man at a bar in Stratford. The older guy was one of the suspicious persons I tailed. It was noisy. The only things I heard were 'fucking eagle,' 'Choc-a-Bubbies,' and the phrase 'all of them.' You just connected the first two."

"The third sounds kind of biblical."

"Unless he was talking about Choc-a-Bubbies. Oh, and after the Bible line, Lon Crum said, 'I can do that.'"

"Not an angel of destruction. Definitely the candy."

"He did, maybe, mace a security guard and steal bags of money."

"Candy."

"Probably."

"Does Crum live up the gated road?"

"The gated road leads to some kind of compound. I stole into it unperceived."

"In other words, you don't know."

"Right."

"You think he's an unworthy antagonist."

"Hmm. He wasn't the shooter and couldn't be the boss."

"You're rationalizing."

"Think? And yeah, Crum might be the low-hanging fruit."

"Thank you for bringing that dead metaphor to life so close to lunch."

"Sorry."

She nodded toward the window. Maytubby followed her nod and looked at the Ada Municipal Airport entrance across the street. It was marked by an old V-tail Beechcraft Bonanza mounted on a steel pole. "You going up to get a better look at that compound?"

"No leaves now, but the bur oaks up there are pretty dense. Don't know if it would tell me anything." He held out his cell. "Google's photo."

"Oh. Summer."

"Sentinel Vending, huh. I'm curious about the rooster. And also about why someone has to meet Lon Crum in a country bar to talk about product."

"The website has no people, but it does have a street address. South Commerce, by the Confederate cemetery."

"As soon as I talk to Fox, I'll go poke around down there."

"Who will you be?"

"Thinking bougie OU frat boy ten years down the road. Resigned but not hopeless. Flannel shirt. Khakis no pleats. Doc Martens."

She laid her hand on his chest and smiled sadly. "Boomer Sooner."

CHAPTER 16

When the Lighthorse dispatcher buzzed Maytubby into headquarters, she motioned him to her desk. She was looking over his shoulder. "Just keep facing me, Bill," she said.

"Okay, Sheila."

She nodded and smiled at someone or some people behind him. When she buzzed the lock, he turned and saw Chief Fox holding the door for a young woman and a young man, both in navy blazers. The man was very short and muscular and had a shaved bullet head. The woman was also fit. She wore her thick black hair cut straight just below her collar. When all three were outside, Maytubby said, "How long they been with Fox?"

"Half hour. Not very long."

"Young."

"I know. Even younger than you. I've been around since the chain-smoking guys in string ties."

"How were they?"

She shrugged. "I had to take up smoking for a while so I could, you know …" She pantomimed one hand burning the other as it approached her breast.

He nodded.

"But most of them didn't do that." She buzzed Fox back in.

In the chief's office, Fox sat beneath the photo of the amiable and impassive governor. The reflected screen of his computer was blank. He said, "Agents Tillis and Sanchez told me to thank the Lighthorse officer for a lead from a guy on Whiskey Lane, south of the casino."

"Did the guy give them my name?"

"No. He called you an 'Indian policeman.' They didn't ask for a name. Why did you tip your hand?"

"To show my goodwill and generosity."

"And to make them think you weren't even playing cards."

"Tillis and Sanchez have anything?"

"Another security camera caught the pickup going west on Seventy. And you know it went south and then back east on Whiskey. The agents are interviewing citizens along that road. They've interviewed the guards at the casino and the guards from the armored car. Someone called the US attorney and claimed he saw a man with a pirate mask driving a white pickup in Krebs."

"Two hours east."

"Reckon that mask might have come off a little this side of Krebs?"

"That's all they have?"

"All they told me. Any leads on the rustlers?"

"I'm combing the range, Chief."

Fox frowned and nodded. He stood and reached to shake Maytubby's hand. For a split second, Maytubby didn't understand what his boss was doing, it had been so long since they last shook hands. He quickly recovered and grasped Fox's hand. Fox let go and turned toward his dark computer screen.

*   *   *

After delivering a summons in Ravia, Hannah Bond drove to the middle of a long straightaway on Oklahoma 1, pulled over, and backed her cruiser into a gravel patch beside a red cedar. Southbound drivers couldn't see her. She could usually bag a day's nonquota of speeders in a few hours.

While she was writing her third citation—a lucrative twenty-over—a white Crown Vic with dash strobes pulled onto the shoulder behind her cruiser. She looked up from her pad of tickets and recognized Scrooby. He got out of his OSBI cruiser, walked away from the highway, and leaned against a jutting rock. When Bond finished with the speeder, she tossed her citation holder in her cruiser, walked over to the far edge of the right-of-way, and stood next to Scrooby. She looked down at him. Her head and hat threw his face into shadow. He tugged at his collar.

"Why didn't you tell me about Alice Lang's involvement in the Richard James case?"

"Because when we was eating hamburgers, I never had heard of it."

"You were one of her best friends. You could have saved me a day."

Bond took out her cell, brought it near her face, and squinted as she typed with her large thumbs.

"What are you doing?" Scrooby said.

The agent's phone began playing "Sweet Home Alabama." He took it out and swiped it.

"I sent you Cathy Barker's number. She's a retired Supreme Court justice for the Chickasaw Nation. She knew Alice before I did, and she knows about the case. Alice never said anything to me about it. I guess it wasn't none of my business."

He put his phone away and looked up. The sun was full in his eyes.

She had walked back to her cruiser and left him leaning against his rock.

CHAPTER 17

An hour after leaving Lighthorse headquarters, Maytubby was sitting in his '65 Ford pickup at a stoplight on Commerce Street in Ardmore, watching the flags over the Oklahoma Veterans Center crack in a stiff north wind. The center was built early in the past century as a Confederate veterans' home, owing much to the Chickasaw Chapter of the United Daughters of the Confederacy. A little farther down Commerce, he passed the Confederate cemetery where his great-great-great-grandfather Maytubby, who rode with Nail's Company in Shecoe's Chickasaw Battalion, was buried.

Sentinel Vending occupied a small concrete-block warehouse with a blue metal mansard roof in the front. Its red, white, and blue acrylic sign featured the company's logo, a generic nineteenth-century soldier in a plumed shako, standing at attention with a bayonet-fixed rifle on his shoulder. Maytubby drove a few blocks past the business, then came back down the alley and parked behind an adjacent business. He took out his cell phone and pretended to stare at its dark screen. A white box truck with the Sentinel logo was backed into the company's warehouse. Maytubby was close enough to see a man loading boxes into the truck. The man was too short and too thin to be Crum.

From thirty yards away, the familiar candy and chip logos on most of the sealed boxes were clear enough. Other logos were unfamiliar, though they were clearly logos. But when the loader moved to the other side of the warehouse, obscured by the freight truck, the boxes he brought to the truck were old and stained and had numbers printed on them in black marker. After those mostly square boxes, he began to load odd-shaped boxes, some of them long and thin. About the size of hard-shell rifle or shotgun cases, Maytubby thought. He powered on his cell camera and slid it to video, held its lens against the driver's window with his shoulder as he drove slowly on down the alley, both hands on the wheel.

Before he entered the Sentinel storefront, he slipped on some tortoise-shell reading glasses, checked his flannel shirt and khakis, his old Doc Martens. He settled a twill OU baseball cap over his thick black hair. In this part of the state, the cap was a cloak of invisibility. The one he left at home, with the letters in Cherokee, not so much.

The plate glass of what was once a showroom had been covered from the inside with reflective window film. Maytubby watched himself walk toward the front door. He recognized none of the vehicles in the reflected parking lot as he walked behind them, memorizing their Oklahoma plates. A small sign under an intercom box said, PUSH TO TALK. The door was buzzed open before he lifted his hand.

A short, thin pokerfaced man, middle-aged, smelling of cigarettes, stood behind the counter. "Can I help you?" he said. He didn't seem to want to. Maytubby heard the pipe-clink of a hand truck in the garage.

A male voice behind a closed office door raged in Hitlerian cadences. Behind the counter were three other office doors, all closed but one, which stood slightly ajar.

Maytubby adjusted his low-power glasses and looked at the counterman. "Folks in my office 'bout to come to blows over their coffee. Everybody drinks it; nobody wants to make it. The helpful people feel put-upon—"

"How many employees?"

"Eleven."

The man stared straight past Maytubby's shoulder as he reached under the counter, pulled out a ring binder, flipped the binder open, and spun it around. When the man bent and set his index finger on a glossy page, the ranter's door swung open. The man at the counter explained something, but Maytubby was watching the screaming man. His crimson face and neck, undeniably roosterish, bobbed ghoulishly. He wiped his mouth with his forearm as he glared at Maytubby. Then he stalked down the hall toward the warehouse.

"I'm sorry," Maytubby said, shaking his head. He looked down at a photo of a small coin-operated coffee machine. "Could you repeat that?"

"This is the forty-two-eighty. We can install the machine and connect it to a water source. Somebody still has to replace the coffee bags. We deliver fresh bags when we empty the coin bin."

Maytubby saw no copy machine along the counter. "Could I have a copy of this page?"

The counterman didn't answer but clicked open the binder rings and took the page into one of the offices with closed doors. Though Rooster had closed the warehouse door, that didn't muffle his rant. Maytubby, who had his hands in his pocket and was staring at the ceiling as he edged down the counter, distinctly heard him rage-yodel, "Drop that fucking alley door, you shit-ass."

Maytubby sidled along the counter until he could see, through the one gapped door, a man's hand holding a cell phone. Then the counterman brought the closed binder and the photocopied page and stood between Maytubby and the door. He took a pen from his pocket and wrote something on the copy, then slid the binder under the counter. Still looking over Maytubby's shoulder, he said flatly, "That's the installation price and the monthly payment."

Because the counterman did not make eye contact, Maytubby tried to look away from his face toward the door. But the instant he did, the counterman looked at his eyes, and Maytubby flicked his eyes back in time to see the counterman look away. Though the pokerfaced man was not familiar to Maytubby, something about his eyes—not their heavy lids, but a lurking smugness—stirred a ripple. "Thank you," Maytubby said as he held up the copy and shook it a little. This bought him a split second to look through the door gap. He saw a face that meant nothing to him. The counterman compressed his lips and nodded slightly before turning away. Rooster had fallen silent and did not return. Maytubby folded the page noisily—and slowly, so he could record every detail of the vendor's office as he turned toward the door. The wall bore dark rectangles where frames had once hung. Not a lamp or a piece of furniture—the inverse of Sentinel's line of food-vending machines, with their big inviting windows, bright lights, and ranks of gaudy packages. Either someone had taken great pains to make the place look uninhabited, or it wasn't ever really inhabited.

There was no way to tell how long it would take Shit-Ass to load the box truck. Maytubby took off his cap and glasses, stopped by Veggies for a takeout box of vegetable lo mein, and then parked near his ancestor's grave, on a hillside with a good view of the alley behind Sentinel. While the garage door remained closed, he wound noodles around a wooden fork and read tombstones. JOHN MUNDT, CO. C, 31ST MISSISSIPPI. ANDREW SALLEE, FORREST'S CAVALRY. Maytubby didn't read his forebear's marker, which bore his own name. He wondered again whether this man had owned Jill Milton's ancestors. And again told himself that was unlikely. A little work at the Holisso Research Center in Sulphur might put that issue to rest. Neither he nor his fiancée had darkened the archive's door.

The five-second video from his cell added nothing but captured the boxes' numbers and a fleeting image of the loader—no one Maytubby recognized. On his cell, through a state portal, he ran the plates on all five vehicles in the Sentinel lot and then matched them with drivers' licenses. None of the photos was of the four men whose faces he had seen in the building, but Lon Crum owned the fifth, the old pickup from Onan's. So nobody but Crum drove his own vehicle to work? Maytubby ran all the owners' names and found nothing but a few traffic violations.

Winding some noodles with his wooden fork, he looked at his right hand and frowned. The counterman had written the coffee machine's price with his left hand. Maytubby had trained himself to resist the tyranny of focus. Rooster, the boxes, the man in the second office—they had blinded him. He gave the counterman a second look. Clean-shaven, lean nose, long upper lip, strong cheekbones. Wheat complexion. The neck muscles, if they were there, didn't show. No satyr tat. No wedding ring. Maytubby had been staring at the ceiling when the counterman walked to the copier, and so didn't see whether he had a pronate roll in his gait. Never smiled—never showed his teeth.

In the surveillance video, the shooter's eyes were not hooded, but wide with excitement, except when he blinked at the shot. Was that shadow of smugness there, even at the distance of the lens? Maytubby imagined the counterman's face with a mouthful of gnarled brown teeth. The picture made the hair on the back of his neck stand up. He let his eyes go unfocused on the prairie sky until the face found its context. When Maytubby was in college at St. John's in Santa Fe, this person had been his landlord's handyman. Maytubby's tiny apartment in a shabby old fake-adobe warren, like all the other apartments in the warren, was a patchwork of wires and pipes and fixtures, some dating back a century. Maytubby replaced fuses and fixed the toilet, but when a more difficult repair was needed, the slightly younger version of the counterman appeared at his door, silent as Bartleby but not so pale, a faint smirk in his eyes, a little metal toolbox in his hand. He had been thinner then—almost cadaverous—and whenever he hit a snag in the repair, the death's-head grimace went gargoyle. Making no eye contact, offering no name, moving with forced calm. His manner had not changed. One day, Maytubby called to report a broken outlet, and a different handyman appeared. Bartleby never returned.

Maytubby stared at the descending Sentinel garage door without seeing it. The box truck was far down the alley before he snapped into the present, set his Veggies carton on the floor, and started his pickup.

CHAPTER 18

"You're on a tail, Bill. Even if your target is big as a hay barn. Like I said, the computer jockeys at OSBI can handle that swindler's bank tricks. Call you later." Bond ended the voice mail. She microwaved a sloppy joe at Big Red's Trading Post in Ravia and ate it as she drove slowly down Greasy Bend Road. Before the old truss bridge came into view, a plume of dust rose, bending with the wind. Jeff Lang's truck shot around the curve, slowed a little as he passed her, like any car passing a cruiser. This time, he avoided eye contact. No pursuit appeared, but as the bridge loomed through bare trees, she saw an OSBI cruiser parked beside the approach.

A young agent Bond didn't recognize knelt at the center of the span, near a guardrail. Bond walked onto the bridge, watching gaps where planks were missing. The agent turned her head, then turned it more to find Bond's face. "You find that nine casing?" Bond said.

"How'd you know about that?"

"I told Scrooby where to find it." Bond paused. "Anybody find her fake boobs?"

"Excuse me?"

"I saw one hung up in the marsh a day ago, took a picture of it for you guys. Probably in Shreveport by now.

The agent stared.

"You find any blood?"

"Haven't looked for it yet. I don't think I should discuss the investigation."

Bond drummed on the belt pouch holding the torn glove. She shrugged. "Whatever." She looked down the Washita. "Did you see that clown pickup just now, big tires?"

The agent sat back on her haunches. "Yeah. I parked next to it when I came. Guy driving it was standing in the middle of the bridge."

"Sweet-smellin' fellow?"

"Somebody else."

Bond nodded slowly.

"Reeked like a sty, didn't he?"

"Yes, he did. Wasn't happy to see me, either. Turned his face away when he passed me."

"Did you a favor. Good luck with your crime scene."

The agent bent to her work, and Bond looked down the river as she walked to her cruiser. Before she got in, she surveyed the mess under the bridge: vodka bottles, beer cans, filthy blankets, condom wrappers. Bond knew that it didn't matter whether Alice had died here or in an art museum, but the trash seemed personal.

She had come to Greasy Bend to think on Jeff Lang, but she didn't expect the first thought she had: he would have made a mess in his aunt's house, and he would have stunk up the place.

Some hours later, after facing down two angry yard dogs to post an eviction notice, Bond heard squawking on her cruiser's radio. She continued to face the snarling dogs while she opened the car door behind her. Sheriff Magaw was saying her name. She clicked on her shoulder radio. "Bond," she said.

"Could you stop by the jail pretty quick?"

"Fifteen," she said. "If I'm not dog meat."

"Roger."

On Bullet Prairie Road, she saw a tow truck winching Jeff Lang's truck up its tilted bed. She stopped and rolled down her passenger window.

"Hey, Hannah."

"Garn."

"Had a little action a few minutes ago. State agent and Sheriff Magaw escorted the owner of this high-performance luxury vehicle to the business end of Tish."

"I'm headed there myself."

"This about the Lang woman?"

"About to find out."

When Bond opened the door to the interrogation room, Jeff Lang glowered at her. He breathed heavily, and his eyes were moist. The room reeked of vomit. Scrooby and Sheriff Magaw sat across from one another.

As Bond sat opposite Lang, Magaw looked at his felt Western hat on the table. He pinched its brim and slid the hat back and forth. "This man—he's waived his rights—says you are the reason he's here. Agent Scrooby and I know that's not true, but we don't know why he thinks it is. Do you know him?"

"He's Alice Lang's nephew."

"Have you talked to him lately?"

"Yesterday morning. I went to his house and told him about his aunt."

"That ain't all you done, looks like." Lang wagged his head at Scrooby and Magaw. "Deputy, you are a regular angel of shit."

"Be quiet," Magaw said.

Lang looked at Bond and smirked. "I bet you and her was quar for each other."

Scrooby glanced at Bond. She stared at the wall. "That's enough of that, Lang. Deputy Bond, let's step into the hall a second."

Before the door closed behind them, Lang shouted, "Why'd you shoot her, Deputy? She screwin' another dyke?"

Scrooby and Bond walked to the end of the hall.

Scrooby looked up at her. "Hannah, did you know Alice Lang was giving money to her nephew?"

"Did you find the neat ledger under 'J' in the oak filing cabinet?"

"Wh ...?"

"Her house was a mess, right? Mud on the floor, chairs knocked over. After that yahoo in there got done dragging her out?"

Scrooby inhaled and blinked. "No. Her house was spotless."

Bond nodded. "Smelled like puke, though."

"Actually, it smelled like—"

"Pine-Sol. Nobody used it to wash down that scene, if that's what you're thinking. She cleaned everything with it, right down to her garden rake."

"You didn't ..."

"A person like that, they like sunshine. All the blinds up and curtains back. That what you found?"

Scrooby frowned. "We found the payment records in the file, and a coil of freshly cut sisal rope in Lang's pickup. And a prior for assault. You made that arrest, Hannah."

"You're barkin' up the wrong tree."

"Do you know which tree I should bark up?" Scrooby said.

"No. You got the science kit."

Scrooby frowned. "We're still waiting on some things. We may have to release him for now—don't want to charge him before we've got a lock on it."

She put on her campaign hat. "But I'll tell you, if you keep barking up that tree, he'll shit on your face. It's what a yahoo does."

CHAPTER 19

Maytubby kept three cars between himself and the Sentinel box truck, but he was close enough, at the first stoplight, to see in the box truck's side mirrors that Shit-Ass had a passenger, and, at the second stoplight, that the passenger was Rooster.

Traffic thinned after the last tract of ranch houses, and Maytubby dropped far behind the Sentinel truck as it rolled northwest toward the Arbuckles. Bay High School was the first building in the first little town. Shit-Ass braked and steered the truck into the school parking lot. The lot not reserved for teachers was full, though the school day had ended a half hour ago. Maytubby stayed on the highway but noticed that the truck double-parked behind Jill Milton's forest-green Honda Accord. He drove around the block and parked behind the school, pulled on a plain khaki cap, and left his specs on the seat.

Rooster wheeled out of the cab, flicked his cigarette onto the Accord's windshield as he took broad, quick strides to the front door. In his fist, he clutched some yellow papers.

If this were just a restock, someone would already have product on a hand truck. Maytubby walked into the school with his head down, hands in his pockets. From the foyer, he could see into the cafetorium, where a dozen or so adults were seated at tables. Jill sat with three other people at a smaller table on a riser. Rooster mounted the stage.

Maytubby caught Jill's attention. Her eyes widened for second; then she frowned and raised one eyebrow. Maytubby pretended to scratch his upper lip, as in "mum," and she nodded and rolled her eyes toward the red-faced man. Maytubby nodded. He walked to the middle of the room and took a seat, nudging an abandoned backpack on the floor. Some people looked at him.

On the dais, a middle-aged woman in a blue blazer rose and thanked the parents for their attendance. The principal, Maytubby guessed. To Rooster, she said, "And thank you for coming, Mr. ...?"

He didn't fill in the blank but stood in a defiant slouch.

She pointed to an empty place at the table. "Won't you have a seat?"

"I'm a businessman. I don't have time to sit around and dis*cuss*. I have to make the money that pays you to do that."

"We all pay taxes, sir." To the assembly she said, "This gentleman is from Sentinel Vending. The high school is in the second year of a two-year contract with Sentinel for all the vending machines on campus. As you know, the school administration and the PTA have been dis ... *exploring* ways to offer our students healthier food choices. We also want to thank Dr. Jill Milton." She motioned Jill to stand. "Dr. Milton is a medical nutritionist with the Chickasaw Nation. She comes to us through the generosity of the nation." There was polite applause.

Maytubby watched the Rooster, whose small yellow eyes were fastened on Jill.

"Right now," the principal said, "there are not many healthy choices in the school's vending machines. Our food service has made a good-faith effort in the last year to serve a more nutritious breakfast and lunch. But between meals—and sometimes instead of them—students migrate to the machines. The drinks are mostly sugary, and the food is mostly candy and chips. We wanted to ask Sentinel what sorts of healthier products could be stocked in the machines." She took her seat and looked at the Rooster. He made his tiny eyes even smaller, thrust the papers forward, and snarled, "This contract you signed doesn't say a damned thing about what we sell. We can sell anything but liquor and dope. We're an Oklahoma business, not some damn San Francisco fairy granola wagon." He turned toward the parents. "If your kids are fat, it's because they eat too much. That's *your* fault. Candy and chips don't turn children into pigs." He thrust his chin toward the panel. "Oh, I can stock raisins and turnip chips, but I'll go broke and you won't get any cheerleader uniforms."

The room fell silent. As the Rooster turned to go, Jill said, "Excuse me."

He spun on his heel and jabbed a finger at her. "You've got no business here, girlie. You don't work here, and your kids don't go to school here. You've got no business in any of these schools out here." He swept his arm. "You're sticking your nose where it doesn't belong."

"In less than a month," she said dryly, "the USDA's Competitive Foods Rule goes into effect, whether I'm here or not. Most of the snacks in your machines right now exceed both the sugar and calorie limits—"

"Sugar and calorie limits," he minced. "You are confusing me with someone who gives a crap about government rules. Hell, you're not even from my American government. That's a sorry enough government, but here you are, a female from an Indian tribe, telling me what I can and can't sell in my own country. I'm going to look into you. You say you're from an Indian tribe, but you don't look like any Indian I ever saw. You look like—"

The principal jumped to her feet, knocking over her chair. "That's enough. You are done here, Mr. Candy Machine."

She was used to being obeyed. When the Rooster faced her full on and took a half step in her direction, power drained from her face. Then he glared at Jill. Maytubby tensed and shifted to the edge of his chair. The Rooster stood still a few seconds—just long enough to make his point—and then rapidly left the stage. All heads turned to follow him. When Maytubby was sure the man's eyes were fixed on the exit, he yanked down the bill of his cap and nudged the backpack into the aisle with his foot.

The pointed toe of Rooster's Western boot caught a shoulder strap on the pack, and he pitched onto the buffed linoleum, his long limbs flailing and whacking furniture. "Fuck fuck *fuck*!" he bellowed, scrambling to get to his feet. Maytubby turned in his seat but kept the bill over his eyes. Jill told him later that the Rooster was ready to rumble until he saw what tripped him.

The hush that had fallen over the room was just giving way to excited chatter when Maytubby banged through a side exit door, jumped a fence, and sprinted to his pickup. The Sentinel truck was backing onto the highway.

It was a big target, so he could give it a long lead. It continued north, toward the buffalo hump of the Arbuckles, stopping at several schools for Shit-Ass to wheel in boxes of product. The Rooster stayed in the truck and smoked. When the colossal wind turbines ranked along the range's south face glowed with late sunlight, the box truck turned off the highway onto a rocky dirt road that climbed through a stand of towering white turbines into rough foothills.

Maytubby took the next turnoff, rumbled over a cattle guard onto private land, and eased the Ford up a steep trail. Between stands of red cedar, he could see the top of the box truck below him, swaying slowly a few hundred yards away. He scanned the road up several switchbacks and saw another white vehicle—a utility van with the Sentinel logo—idling in a turnout.

He parked behind a granite boulder, grabbed his binoculars, and watched the box truck pull alongside the van and stop. This time, the Rooster got out of the truck. The van's driver door opened, and the bulk of Lon Crum listed in the driver's seat. Rooster shouted something, and Crum scrambled to the road, the tail of his uniform shirt twisted and fanned like a kilt. All three men disappeared behind the vehicles. Maytubby backtracked on foot, in the hill's shadow, behind a defile of bastard oaks. Though it was winter, he watched for rattlesnakes.

The sun was behind him, so it wouldn't glint off his field glasses. He trained them on the three men hustling boxes from the big truck to the van. These were the tattered boxes numbered with Magic Marker. When they finished, Crum slammed the van's rear doors. The Rooster suddenly spun around and looked right into Maytubby's binocular lenses. Maytubby didn't flinch but looked straight into his feral little eyes. The Rooster spun just as suddenly the opposite way and cursed at Lon Crum, who ducked and then lurched to his cab.

Twenty minutes later, Maytubby was parked behind the same patch of blackjack oaks near Ardmore Municipal where he had waited for the quarry biker. Just inside the airport gate, Crum's van had taxied alongside a parked, running van, an old one, crudely stenciled with GILL JANITORIAL. Both drivers got out and opened the rear doors of their vans. Maytubby used the zoom on his phone to photograph them. When they had moved all Crum's boxes to old Gill, the young driver of old Gill, who was wearing what appeared to be an olive uniform shirt and matching pants, handed two small USPS-looking boxes—white with red and blue stripes—to Crum. As the driver turned to go, Crum cradled both packages in one arm and grabbed the driver by his shoulder. Crum then took a small notebook from his uniform pocket and held it to the driver's face. The driver took the notebook and held it close to his face—affectedly, Maytubby thought. The driver was shaking his head slowly. More bad acting. He shrugged and searched the back of his van, retrieved a third box, smaller than the others, and handed it to Crum.

"*All of them*," Maytubby said, the vapor of his breath fogging the windshield. Mr. Volvo didn't trust this middleman but didn't want to make the swap himself.

Crum drove east on State 53, just south of the airport. A spanking new Embraer twin prop, not thirty feet above his van, yawed on its final approach to correct for a slight crosswind. Maytubby followed Crum across the Washita and north on US 177. It was clear where this was going, and Maytubby was grateful for a short winter day—the sentry at the compound on Powell Road knew his pickup. A bright moon, though, he might outwit.

At the top of the last hairpin, he turned off his headlights and drove on around the hillside. Through his binoculars, he watched Crum's headlights slide toward the turnoff and then strike two vehicles at the gate—the guard's blue Dakota pickup and the silver Volvo SUV.

Someone walked twice in front of Crum's headlights. There wasn't time to transfer the big boxes. The smaller boxes seemed more important. Crum then pulled into the drive and backed onto Powell Road.

"*Uhk*," Maytubby said, throwing the field glasses on the seat. He jammed the column shifter into reverse and fishtailed up the tight curve. Crum didn't seem like someone who would question a cloud of dust when there was no wind and nobody had passed him going the other way. There were no passive reverse lights on the old truck, so he was searching for a turnout by moonlight, struggling to keep the truck as far as he could from the outside embankment without striking the hill on the inside. The truck briefly slipped into a bar ditch, and saplings shrieked along metal.

Maytubby glanced out the front windshield, saw Crum's headlight shafts cutting through dust. When Maytubby turned around, he glimpsed a hurtling form in the moonlight. The young buck lit with a clunk in the pickup bed, lost its footing, fell, and slid against the cab. "Shit!" Maytubby said. As the buck struggled to regain its legs, it blocked the cab's rear window. Maytubby slowed to a stop. The deer clattered around in the bed for a few seconds, then bounded into the brush. Switching on his headlights, Maytubby drove toward Crum and then passed him, slowly, with little room to spare. He could not see in the van's tinted windows. At the first drive cut, he turned around and tailed Crum seven miles to a small cinder-block cottage set back from the road and partly hidden by cedars. Maytubby remembered that it was unpainted. Likely, it was once the milk house for a big frame house long gone to dust. Now it stood alone on the mile between section lines.

Crum still had boxes of something that didn't belong in vending machines. Give him an hour. There was no natural cover for the whole mile. Somebody, probably not Crum, had chosen this place well—another reason to wait, but it meant looping through tracts of low-end vacation homes on Lake of the Arbuckles. Minnow Pause, Hasteys' Retreat, Buggses Rug. For night visitors, each drive was marked by a pattern of reflectors—the Christian cross in all four reflector colors, initials, cattle brands. A few reflective-painted Uncle Sam whirligigs spun madly.

After each loop, Maytubby looked for traffic at the milk house. After his sixth pass by Hastey's Retreat, he saw taillights leaving Crum's driveway. Somebody, probably not Crum, had moved the boxes fast. When the lights were a quarter mile ahead, Maytubby saw they belonged to a black Ford Econoline. He grabbed his field glasses and memorized its New Mexico plates.

Never breaking the speed limit, the Econoline followed old US 77 parallel to the interstate a few miles to Oil City Road, then west. When the road was deep in the country and his truck was conspicuous, Maytubby turned off his headlights. There were few curves. The Econoline turned onto a dirt road that led to Healdton's tiny airstrip. Maytubby stopped in the moonshade of some post oaks and glassed the only structure at the field: a metal hangar with three doors. One sodium lamp shone on the building and pooled on the ground.

The Econoline drove down the runway to the end opposite Maytubby, made a U-turn, and illuminated the runway with its headlights. It faced the north wind, as a landing plane would, so Maytubby searched the sky above it for a landing light. He waited less than fifteen seconds. The light blazed on just a few feet above the van as a single-engine plane, ghostly silent in glide, vaned and floated before scuffing the runway. The landing light quickly went out, as did the Econoline's headlights.

Plane and van met at the edge of the sodium lamplight. Maytubby recognized the craft as a 1969 Mooney Mustang. He memorized its registration number, which ended in "E"—*Echo*. The plane's DeLorean hatch levitated. The pilot stayed put while the van driver stacked boxes in the plane. Less than a minute after it had landed, the Mooney was taxiing to the south end of the runway. Its landing light shone for only a few seconds, until the plane lifted off. Then its faint red and green position lights tilted as it banked west.

Maytubby watched it too long. When he looked for the Econoline's brake lights, they were already at the field's gate. Then they were gone. Even in decent moonlight, Maytubby couldn't see which way the van had turned.

CHAPTER 20

Nichole Hewitt held a wadded tissue to her nose and motioned Maytubby to a chair at her dining table. Her eyes were scalded. "Look at this food from the church," she said, moving her free hand over a dozen casserole dishes crowded on the table. "Five potato salads. The refrigerator is packed. Mom and I ..." She shrugged. And the girls don't like most of this. Onions, pimientos, mustard—some kid repellent in half the dishes. You have to take some for you and Jill."

"How are the girls doing?"

"Natalie is three, you know. Things are different for her, I guess. Ella's a year older, but she has never even had a pet die. She's kind of lost right now." She looked at the floor and bit her nail. "Oh, Bill, I'm afraid Ella won't remember her father." She sobbed into her hands, and Maytubby grasped her shoulder.

"I remember my mother," he said. "I was four."

She looked at him. "Really?"

"Yes," he said. "In spite of my father, who never mentioned her. You will help your children remember Tommy."

"Even that …" Her hands were shaking. "The idea of it …"

"After my dispatcher told me what happened, I drove some miles blind and deaf."

"That's where I still am, way up in the middle of the air. My own children seem far away, in some other dimension almost, even when they're asleep next to me."

"Can you sleep?"

"When I'm exhausted. I sleep and wake at wildly random times. Mom keeps the girls on the regular clock. I think they're a little afraid of me right now." She pointed to her eyes. "And it's hard for me to read to them."

"Grandma isn't the same."

She nodded. "As Tommy, either. He did the voices."

"Nichole, I don't know who did this yet. I've found a circle of men who are engaged in murky enterprises. They may be smugglers."

"Jill told me about the uniforms."

"I don't know if these guys are behind the robbery. The FBI is looking in a different direction."

"They talked to me a few hours ago."

Maytubby laid a hand on the table and looked away. "Tillis and Sanchez."

"They wanted to know if Tommy had told me about anything suspicious at the casino—any shady characters. Or if he was friends with anyone like that. Or if he had a gambling problem. They asked if Tommy was ever out late at night."

"They have to ask those questions, but I don't."

"I was in no mood. I took that picture of the stickball tournament off the wall and showed it to them. I told them he practiced under the lights a lot. The young woman asked what he was doing."

"Didn't do her homework."

"An electrician would case a building he wired—for a den of thieves. Doesn't make a lick of sense."

"No." He looked over the covered dishes on the table. "Any of these have onion, mustard, *and* pimientos?"

"This." She handed him a ruby plastic container with the name Tigner penned on a piece of masking tape.

They stared at the red cube as a fresh norther howled down the Hewitts' chimney.

CHAPTER 21

Hannah Bond paused in the lobby of the Johnston County Courthouse to send the newspaper photo of a young Richard James to her contacts. She stowed her phone and had started toward the front door when the dispatcher's phone lines came alive. "Is anyone hurt?" the dispatcher said. "Okay. I'll send an ambulance." The phone continued to buzz. Bond looked at the dispatcher. "Vehicle-train, Hannah. Kelly Road and the Santa Fe tracks. Possible fatality."

"I'll radio the Highway Patrol on my way."

Bond pushed her cruiser over the deserted straightaway of Oklahoma 1. The sun had almost set, but the high blue light was still strong. Her cell chimed with texts. She ignored it. A Highway Patrol Charger's strobes flashed in her mirror, and the cruiser she had summoned passed her as if she were parked. She saw the knot of cars just before she passed the idling BNSF engine, scraps of metal and upholstery jammed against its steel pilot.

Wreckage lined the rail grade, and tufts of batting swirled like snow. The last tanker car had cleared the grade crossing, where the back half of an old van lay on its side. The panel said, LL JANITORIAL. The front half had been sheared away.

A semicircle of people, including the train's engineer, stood at the crossing, looking down into the drainage ditch. Bond recognized that formation. Only the state policeman descended the gravel. Then he stopped halfway down. Bond knew that, too. The patrolman she recognized, Jake Renaldo. She joined him, and they stared at a headless corpse, its legs bent over the shoulders. It was clothed in a dark green civilian uniform.

"The head's over on this side," said a man on the tracks.

"Hannah," Renaldo said, nodding. "Broad daylight, no excuse for chicken."

"He didn't try to beat the train," said a panting man in a yellow safety vest. Bond and Renaldo looked up.

"You're the engineer," Bond said. "Conductor still on the train."

"Yeah. Son of a bitch in a big white pickup pushed that van onto the tracks. I couldn't believe it." His voice shook. He kept his eyes on the officers and out of the ditches. An ambulance siren lifted over the prairie. "There's no lights or gates out here. When the van stopped, I relaxed and laid off the horn. Started looking further down the tracks. Then this white pickup turned off the highway and pulled up behind the van, real close, stopped. I didn't think nothing about it. I wasn't three seconds out when that pickup's big old grille smacked the van's tail and sent the cab onto the tracks. I don't think the van driver had his foot set on the brake. The pickup was already backing away when the pilot hit the van."

"You see the pickup driver's face?" Bond said.

The engineer colored and looked at the darkening sky. He looked like bottled mayhem. "No," he spat.

"You came from his passenger side; you were up high."

"Uh, yeah. Right."

"You just guessing it was a man because of the truck?"

"No. I saw his hairy fucking hands."

Renaldo turned toward the half-dozen bystanders, who were walking toward their vehicles. One man leaned against the crossing sign pole and vomited. Renaldo said, "Any of you-all witness this crash?"

They all shook their heads and looked at the others to see whether there was a witness.

Johnston County EMS wheeled onto the grade crossing, followed by Garn's tow truck and the sheriff's accident investigation team. Bond led the engineer to the team and returned to Renaldo.

"Happened to him before, I can tell," Renaldo said. "Young as he is. Afraid he's got the curse."

"What curse?" Bond said.

"Too many of those," Renaldo nodded at the van, "for it to be just bad luck."

Bond looked up the track. "Bullshit."

Renaldo nodded to himself and walked back to his cruiser.

Hannah turned on her phone. Most of her local contacts had messaged that they didn't recognize James' face.

* * *

Bond was frying three eggs and a pork chop, listening to a police scanner, when Maytubby called. "Your embezzler has a little hipster soul patch now," he said.

"Where's he at?"

"State Fifty-Three, next-to-last driveway eastbound before the railroad tracks and the Ardmore airport entrance. White-and-gray mobile home. Clothesline, little broken red pickup. He drives a yellow Suzuki dirt bike with saddlebags and a stolen plate to X-Silica by Mill Creek."

"I guess you weren't fetching my water before you got the text."

"No."

"I should of texted you the picture yesterday. Outdoor work, huh?"

"Unless he wears coveralls to the office."

"Felony embezzlement can get you throwed off the inside-job list. Hard to embezzle glass sand."

"You think he was working alone?"

"Cathy Barker worked a little on this case. She told me the restitution checks were steady. All from the same Tulsa bank."

"And you said he had a good attorney. So you're thinking cahoots."

"Pack of thieves robbing the Golden Play. You're following James you must be thinking that, too."

"Morning after the robbery, a propane jockey saw a pickup like the casino getaway truck drop a man at this trailer. I watched the guy a little, followed him to the quarry. Hoping he might stop at this place on Powell Road I've been watching. Sketchy folks, moving stuff in trucks and planes. But he went on by to the quarry."

"Powell Road would suit a band of desperadoes."

"Some of the trucks belong to Sentinel Vending in Ardmore."

"Any of 'em belong to L. L. Janitorial?"

"It's Gill Janitorial."

"Then the first two letters of Gill's name are wrapped around a Santa Fe freight engine on Kelly Road."

"What?"

"You been away from your Lighthorse radio."

"I'm in the 'sixty-five."

"Engineer said the old janitor van was stopped at the crossing and some dude in a late-model white F-One-Fifty Supercab with a black grille guard—same as the Golden Play truck—pushed him in front of the engine. Van driver was decapitated."

"You see what was in the van?"

"Didn't look close. Lot of janitor stuff out on the ground—buffer, mops, yellow buckets. Not what you wanted to hear."

"If this is the same van, whoever was driving it last night met one of my sketchy people at the Ardmore airport and gave him some packages. Not enough, apparently. My guy challenged him, and he handed over one more."

"Your guy wasn't in a white One-Fifty."

"Sentinel van."

"Jake called in the description. Still no tag. He said there was going to be an uprising if a fourth of the men in the county are pulled over twice in three days."

"No witness besides the engineer and the conductor?"

"Jake asked nice. Ever'body said no. Except a guy who was barfing. He kind of shook his head."

"Pickup go north or south?"

"North."

"Tough customers, Hannah. Maybe we should leave this to the professionals."

"Huh."

* * *

Bond plated her supper and stood over the table, holding the skillet. She still wore her uniform. The Ardmore airport was not far as the crow flies, but the crow used to fly over Greasy Bend bridge before it was closed. The work-around was long. She wanted to drive her old Skylark to the embezzler's trailer that minute, but what would she do when she got there? She imagined kicking in his door and dragging him outside.

The scanner erupted. Bond ignored it until she heard a pursuit description of Jeff Lang's pickup. The pursuing officers, in separate cruisers, were deputies called Katz and Eph, a last name and a first—Ephraim. Katz said, "Got*dang*it he don't go over eighty, but he jigs right down the middle like a razorback hog. I'm afraid that boneshaker's gonna fly apart and fill my cruiser full of holes. Phoo-*oo!*"

Bond learned in the next few seconds that the pursuit was approaching her house on the north side of Tishomingo and that the Highway Patrol was rushing to lay down spike strips south of town. She grabbed her coat and duty belt, slapped a portable strobe atop the Skylark, and was outside the city limits in seconds. The tappets in the old Buick's little eight clattered like hail.

At the edge of the rock prairie, the cyclops topped a small hill. It wove slightly from side to side on the two-lane highway. Bond didn't know which headlight she was looking at, but it didn't matter. She calmly drove straight at it as fast as the Skylark would carry her. She flashed her brights a few times and then, for three seconds, turned her headlights off altogether. Hannah Bond seldom strayed from her pursuit training. But when she did …

Jeff Lang's feeble horn dopplered toward her. She matched his swerves and slowed a bit to stay nose-to-nose, like a sheepdog. He swerved less and less and approached the Skylark head-on. She glimpsed his frozen grimace an instant before he veered off the road. Katz and Eph parted to avoid her. A third cruiser followed Katz. Bond made a noisy bootleg U-turn. By driving in the bar ditch, she struck the path of Lang's truck before the others and followed it over a downed fence into a rocky pasture. Lang struck a boulder, and his monster rear tires bucked high and then came down hard.

Bond ran to the truck, reached up to open the driver's door, grabbed Lang by his sweatshirt collar, and pulled him from the cab. She grabbed both his arms behind his back, kicked his legs loose, and let him fall. The fog from their panting swirled in headlight beams. Bond heard footsteps behind her. "Cuffs!" she called. A pair appeared, and she put them on Jeff Lang, who grunted and writhed.

"Phoo-*oo,* Hannah!" Katz said. "You appeared out of the night like some kind of meteor!"

Bond stood. She looked at Eph, who was holding his pistol loosely and pointing it in her general direction. "Holster that gun, Deputy," she barked. "You're going to shoot somebody." He stared at the pistol for a second before doing as he was told.

"Why are you chasing Jeff Lang?"

"Here comes the man," Katz said.

Bond spotted the OSBI cruiser before she recognized Scrooby, puffing as he mounted the rise.

"Hannah wants to know why we're chasing this guy," Katz said.

Scrooby frowned at Lang, then looked at Bond. "I want to know what *you're* doing at this party."

"Why, she run him off the road before we got to Tish, Agent," Katz said. "She got the balls of a Brangus bull."

Scrooby stopped far enough away from the group so he wouldn't have to look up at Bond.

"I heard the pursuit on my scanner," Bond said.

"We tightened our case and attempted to arrest Lang in Wapa-nucka," Scrooby said. "For his aunt's murder."

"He fled," Eph said. Bond and Scrooby looked at him.

Scrooby said, "Lang was in possession of a Glock nine, a recently cut length of sisal rope matching the rope around his aunt's wrists. He was his aunt's sole heir, even though they didn't get along. An agent recently saw him loitering near the scene of the crime. One thing he was not in possession of was an alibi."

"I'm fucking freezing over here!" Nobody looked at Lang. "Get me in a damned car!"

Katz looked directly at Eph and yelled, "Deputy Bond's car is nice and warm."

"You got ballistics on the nine?" Bond said.

When Scrooby didn't answer, she said, "You find any matching prints at Alice Lang's house?"

After a few seconds of Quaker meeting, Eph said, "I'll take him into Tish."

"Meet you there," Scrooby said, and walked away.

"Deputy, you got any Little Trees in your prowler?" Katz said.

"It's against regulations," Eph said.

"Worth a write-up. Shit, worth a demotion. That guy was in my cruiser once. Phoo-*oo*. I don't imagine Hannah has a spare hanging on her mirror," Katz said to Bond's back—a little louder. She walked to the Skylark, pulled off the strobe, twisted herself into the car, and backed down the hill. Katz elbowed Eph and snickered. "She don't want to share."

CHAPTER 22

The Heartland Flyer was picking up speed out of Ardmore when it blared through the State 53 grade crossing, its passengers' silhouettes streaming across Bond's windshield. She had stopped by her house to change out of her uniform, get her Steiner military binoculars, and bag some pork chops. When the gates lifted, she drove slowly past Richard James' mobile home. The lights were on. She returned to the crossing and parked in Maytubby's grove beside the tracks.

The Steiners were the size of a toolbox and normally required a tripod. Bond held them in one hand while she fished for a chop with the other. For a half hour, she stared through the only uncurtained window at a nearly full bottle of brown spirits, the bottle faceted like an old glass doorknob and corked with a figure she couldn't make out. The thrust reversers of a freight jet roared on the tarmac at Ardmore Municipal behind her. The Skylark's windows fogged, so she rolled one down and let the cold wind in. A train horn blew a ways up the track.

A thin, well-groomed young man with a blond soul patch crossed the kitchen. He wore a uniform like the janitorial van driver's. When he reappeared, he had a quart of milk and an apple. After his snack, he disappeared, then reappeared in the doorway. By the faint light of the airport's sodium lamps, she saw him lock the door, walk around the little red truck, and come directly toward her.

Inside the bright trailer, he could not have seen the car. Now he would. Slowly she lowered the glasses and lay across the tattered bench seat, her face turned, listening for his footstep on the gravel. The train blew again, and her rearview mirror reflected its headlights, flooding the Skylark's interior with light. Though the Skylark was not a cop car and its paint bore forty years of dings and sun, it was in the wrong place.

The first crunch of roadbed gravel was very close. With her left eye, Bond watched through the windshield, expecting to see James' face any instant. Instead, his footfalls accelerated. Then the train blew long for the crossing. Bond sat up. She watched James leap the tracks and disappear down the embankment just before the engine roared past.

If she stayed where she was, she would see only what Maytubby had seen. When the train had cleared the crossing, she had a view of light-plane hangar stalls, one of which was empty. She drove through the airport entrance, down a feeder taxiway, and into the empty stall. She parked in shadow, hung the massive Steiners from her neck, and strode along the hangar's shadow.

Though it was past midnight, the freight terminal was hopping. Semis churned up and down the warehouse approach. Bond made her way to a row of aviation services lining a taxiway apron. Aside from a few out-of-town planes on the tie-down lot, this part of the airport was deserted. She sat on a shadowed bench and swept the freight terminal with the Steiners. A forklift beeped across the dock, and a few workers stood around a stack of empty pallets. Scanning away from the terminal, Bond paused to read the sign on a Quonset hut. CUSTODIAN. It was lettered by an unsteady hand and lit by a single old clamshell light. The hut's transom glowed dully. Snatches of country-and-western music drifted from the warehouse.

The Quonset door opened, and James turned to switch off the light.

A cluster of keys hung from his belt, and he carried a yellow janitor caddy holding some spray bottles. He walked fast away from Bond, toward the freight apron, and disappeared. No sooner had she set the binoculars on her knee than the caddy bounced back into view—James at the quick march. He covered the entrance road so fast, Bond had to walk in the light. He was clearly on a mission, didn't seem interested in anything around him. He pulled his cell phone out, glanced at the screen, and put it back. Bond looked at her watch. 12:14. Coming up on a round minute.

James passed the last hangar before the airport entrance and stopped. Bond edged into shadow and stopped as well. Dust swirled in the amber sodium light. James bent his head and turned his back to the wind. Very soon, headlights appeared on State 53, crossed the railroad. Was it a van, and would it have "Sentinel" painted on the side?

It was, and it did. The driver parked it and left it running while he opened the tailgate. Short, bow-legged fellow. When James pulled packages from his caddy, the driver took them with his left hand and stowed them in the van. After the van drove away, turning toward the Washita and not the way it came, James did not return to the Quonset hut but walked briskly toward his home. Bond gave him fifty yards before she made for the Skylark. She was inside the hangar when James stopped at the place she had been parked near the tracks. Now he did turn around. Without the Steiners, she couldn't tell where he was looking. She was counting the seconds the van had on her. James balanced on a rail a few seconds and then jogged toward his mobile home, the caddy bouncing.

The Skylark was too old to have running lights, so Bond was well on her way to the Washita before James was indoors. At the edge of Gene Autry, she switched on her headlights. The state highway T-boned US 177. Bond grabbed her binoculars to look for taillights both directions, but she hadn't even reached the stop sign when she remembered May-tubby's band of desperadoes on Powell Road. The Skylark shuddered through a sharp left and labored along the Washita for almost half a mile before it reached its top speed, ninety-two. Crooked cedar fence posts flickered at the cusp of her headlights.

On Powell Road, after checking her odometer, Bond kept the van's taillights far in front of her. In a few minutes, the brake lights flashed, pivoted to the right, off the road, and stopped. So the drive was gated. She kept the spot fixed after the van started moving again, away from the road. She slowed as she approached the turnoff, but when a pair of amber reflectors glinted in her headlights, she accelerated. A pickup blocked the gate. "Advertisin'," she said as she looked at the odometer.

Before it again found level ground, Powell Road mounted and then circled a knob. Putting the knob between her and the Sentinel people, she parked and grabbed the Steiners. The barbed-wire property fence sagged because many of its old posts had broken at the ground. Otherwise, Bond would have walked until she found a tree for a stile.

There was still enough moonlight for her to decipher rocks and clumps of yucca. She was over the top of the knob in a few strides. The guard pickup was easy to see, but the driveway grew faint under a canopy of leafless bur oaks. Bond closed her eyes a while to get her night vision, then slowly glassed the trees. Gradually, faint reflections of moonlight gave shape to structures under the trees. Pretty large structures. No need for tractor barns. Not an inch of cultivated soil for miles. And if there were anything valuable in those structures, they would be floodlit. A match flare briefly illuminated an exterior brick wall and silhouetted a man. The glow of his cigarette was too dim to follow.

She watched until the moon set.

CHAPTER 23

"New silver Volvo SUV," Hannah Bond said.

She peeled back the lid of the red cube and examined its contents, resealed the lid, and pushed the box aside. Maytubby, in civvies, sat across from her in the Aldridge Coffee Shop, a densely mirrored survivor from the twenties. Dishes rattled into bus tubs as downtown Ada merchants donned their coats and left to open for the day.

"Now maybe I can return the favor for telling me where the embezzler lays his sorry head. Volvo driver chunky, half bald, fancy clothes?"

Maytubby nodded.

"Pulled him over two days ago, outside Wapanucka. Doing over a hundred. He hit a hawk, and the rabbit the hawk dropped cracked my windshield."

"In keeping with the whole low-profile shell-company program."

"New Volvo SUV in Wapanucka at all. Funny last name. Sounds like 'sumac.' Cache address."

"Courteous, I bet."

"I told him he killed a bald eagle."

Maytubby smiled. A server set a bowl of oatmeal and a portion cup of peanut butter in front of him. Bond scowled at his breakfast and shook her head. "I don't know how you live on that crap." The server returned with Bond's breakfast—a waffle, four rashers of bacon, hash browns, and three eggs over easy. She bit one of the bacon strips in half. While Maytubby was salting his oatmeal, Bond raised her index finger. She swallowed and said, "Sulak. Fred, Frank. Something."

"The guy who brought the packages in the Sentinel van last night—what did he look like?"

"Bandy-legged. Wiry. Short." Bond tore the waffle in two and folded an egg into one half. "He didn't waste energy. Moved real efficient."

"Not the last person who made the same run. Right-handed?"

Bond looked out the window and then down at her hands. She moved the waffle burrito from one hand to the other a few times. Then she held it up in her left and nodded at Maytubby.

"So this guy and Sulak are showing up for graveyard at the Powell Road compound. Tommy Hewitt's shooter was left-handed, short, and bandy-legged. Anything else stand out about the guy? Marks?"

"Too far away."

"Beard?"

"Clean shaved. Like I said, he could do two things at once, had good balance. You got a word."

"Agile."

"That's it. Hard for tall folks. James had a fancy bottle on—"

"Blanton's Single Barrel Bourbon. Jockey on top. Expensive for the boondocks. I saw the cheap stuff in the kitchen, too. What bush is OSBI beating?"

"Alice's stinkpot nephew. He's mean enough but dumb as a stump. And not even in the same county as agile. He would've made a pig's breakfast of killing her."

Maytubby spooned peanut butter into his oatmeal and stirred it in.

Bond said, "I run the nephew off the road for Scrooby last night. Your favorite lawmen was in on the pursuit."

Maytubby looked at her.

"Katz and Eph."

"Phooo-*ooo*."

Bond nodded, then shook her head. "And Eph. That man needs a brain transplant." Then she murdered her waffle burrito. She held up her coffee mug to show the server, put it down, and said, "What does our US government think?"

"Inside job, apparently. Agents asked Nichole Hewitt if Tommy had a gambling problem or if he hung out with sketchy characters."

"Sorry sons a bitches." Bond shook Tabasco on her hash browns. "This stuff tastes good on eggs but nasty on waffles. Somebody called Dispatch in Tish, said before the train wreck she saw a man fiddling with a license plate on the back of a white pickup. Roadside park just down the road from the Kelly crossing. Burly guy. She didn't see his face. Wouldn't give her name. 'Course, it was right on the screen."

"Bar owner I know ID'd the guy who made the airport pickup before the one you saw. He drives a truck for Sentinel. She called me when he came in, and I eavesdropped on a conversation between this guy and your hawk man, Sulak. Now, I think Sulak was telling the guy—his name is Crum—to make sure the janitor wasn't skimming."

"So, 'Crumb' as in bread?"

"C-R-U-M. Crum found out he was and snitched. Sulak, or whoever the boss is, killed him or had him killed, and brought James in off the quarry bench. They can't call him 'Richard' out in Hog Waller. Did Justice Barker ever mention another name?"

"No, but I bet he called him*self* Richard. You know anything about Gill Janitorial?"

"Subcontractor for night services, two years. Stavos Gill signed the papers. Or someone calling himself that. I can't find anyone in the state by that name."

"Stick-out first name. Sounds foreign." Bond mopped the last puddle of yolk with a scrap of waffle and bolted it. She laid a ten on the table and stood. "I better get back across the county line before the damn pow'rs of darkness lay waste to Connerville."

CHAPTER 24

"Thorny died two years ago. Who's this, again?"

"Bill Maytubby. Mr. Tillotson was my landlord when I was at St. John's." Maytubby had parked the pickup at a convenience store in Lawton. He rebound his shabby little address book with a rubber band and stuck it back in his shirt pocket.

"I'm his niece. Nobody ever calls on this old rotary phone. You one of his old hooch buddies?"

"No, ma'am." The old Ford's heater fan soughed.

A Zippo lid clinked. "*Mmnnn*," the niece said. Then she exhaled. "The old dotard loved his Johnnies. Called people his own age 'the Dead.' Maytubby. Sounds like that Faulkner character …"

"Ikkemotubbe."

"God, if you and Thorny were in the room, he would roll his eyes over to me and say, 'You see, Carol, the Dead have no interest in such things. Ikkemotubbe was not a golf celebrity; they are not interested.'"

Maytubby smiled.

"So you are Choctaw—no, wait—Chick, uh, Chickasaw?"

"Half. I'm a tribal police officer." Maytubby heard church bells over the old rotary phone.

"Did Thornton Tillotson have an even darker side I don't know about?"

"I have no idea," Maytubby said. "I was calling about the handyman who worked on my apartment—and others, I assume. He's turned up here in Oklahoma, in fishy circumstances."

"I'm afraid I didn't know any of them by name, though he sent some to my *casita* on Otero before I moved into his house."

"I don't know his name anyway. Short guy, thin as a cattail. Never spoke. But if he hit a glitch in the job, his eyes bulged, and his face got really ..."

"*Twisted.* Oh, my God," Carol said. "And those teeth. Just when I had him good and forgotten."

"Sorry," Maytubby said.

"Oh. Duncan Calls. Last name as in 'several telephone.'" She paused, but Maytubby did not have to write the name. "He's still alive? I read in the *New Mexican* he was thrown from his pickup when it rolled during a pursuit in the Manzanos. Maybe I just assumed he died. That was a good while ago." The church bells stopped ringing.

"He have a lot of trouble with the law?"

She exhaled into the phone. "Even before Thorny hired him. Thorny didn't know he'd done time in Laramie for assault."

"You'd leave that off the handyman résumé."

"You would. One of Thorny's tenants told Calls that his caulking bead was too large. Calls broke the guy's face and disappeared."

"He struck me as volatile."

"Thorny would pet a rabid dog." She whistle-exhaled.

"Do you remember if Calls hung with other people who might have been in trouble with the law?"

"I got nothing. Give me your number."

He did. "I'm sorry about your uncle."

"Me, too. He was a wiseacre."

Maytubby pocketed his phone and bit into the apple he had just bought. He pulled onto Quanah Parker Trailway, shifting with his apple hand. The address on Frank Sulak's license was near the foothills of the Wichita Mountains. Computer images from street and space were taken in summer, and mesquite leaves obscured some of the acreage.

Dayo Mission Road left a knot of ranch houses on its way north through pastureland. Before it made a hard right at the Fort Sill military reservation fence, Maytubby saw a lone mailbox at the head of a dirt driveway. The address Sulak gave was stenciled on the box. There was no gate or cattle guard, so no livestock. Distant artillery boomed on military ranges in the shadow of Mount Scott.

The drive split a stand of mesquite and disappeared over a rise. He donned his OU hat and drove over the rise.

A rusted windmill tower, missing its wind wheel, listed to the north. The tank it once fed was half buried in sand. Fifty yards away, an old residential propane tank nested in dead bluestem grass. No sign of a slab or chain wall. Wind had swept the earth clean of tracks.

Sulak may not have given his real address to the Department of Public Safety, but he could not have randomly matched the five digits on the mailbox. Maybe he owned the land; maybe he lived nearby and knew that the place was uninhabited. Back on the road, Maytubby drove through rolling grassland cut by small streams. A coyote loped parallel to the road, eyeing the pickup.

Maytubby noticed that a sodium streetlamp over a driveway gate had been shot out. This meant nothing except that it was the first damaged one he had seen today. Most of the traffic signs on country roads were slug-pocked. But the next streetlamp, a few hundred yards along, was shot out, and the ones after those two were not. There were no visible houses or buildings, only a double-strand electric fence on the north and a barbed-wire ranch fence, with milled wooden posts, on the south.

Maytubby made a three-point U-turn and drove slowly between the shattered lights, scanning the shallow ditches on both sides of the road. He reached the first light without seeing anything unusual, turned around, and drove more slowly, stopping every few feet. Halfway between the lights, looking south, he noticed a small stretch of fence that looked off. He stared at it for a couple of seconds. All four strands of barbed wire were less taut than the wire on either side. He looked all around to make sure he was alone, put on his camo ball cap. He left the truck with the keys in the ignition, screened from the field by a few mesquites, and walked through the dry ditch to take a closer look.

Nearer the ditch, he could see where tires had flattened the grass. Pinching the top strand of wire, he pulled it toward himself. The two nearest fence posts moved with the wire. They were not planted in the ground. Maytubby went to the first pole that stayed put and discovered that it was split vertically. Loops of baling wire at top and bottom bound the halves together and could be slid off to open the gate. This basic poor-man's gate was common, but Maytubby had never seen one where there was no road or trail, and he had never seen one so painstakingly concealed.

The property was flat and treeless but uncultivated. There were no cow flops. He looked up and saw that there was no electric wire between the lamps. At each lamp, the wire paralleling the road continued perpendicular to the road and away from it. He tilted the half post, stepped through the space, and closed the gate, looping the top wire barely over the top of the post so he could get back through it fast. A quarter mile into the pasture, he found an orange wind sock flattened on the ground by stones. Its frame and short mast, as well as a fat flashlight, lay in a shallow trench next to it.

A few more steps revealed smudged divots cut by what the wind sock told him were the tires of planes landing toward the south, the prevailing wind in most of Oklahoma, though not on this winter day. He walked straight south, pacing off the ballpark landing distance for a Mooney Mustang—about three hundred yards. Then he stopped and parsed the field. Before his eye had traveled a half circle, it was arrested by an off-palette splotch. When he stood over it, he saw a pair of very large camouflage coveralls pinned to the ground with stones. He grabbed the crotch and yanked, spilling the rocks and exposing what looked like three plastic garbage can lids, each with six screws around the circumference. Maytubby knew he was looking at prepper hardware.

He took out his pocketknife and removed all the screws of the first, pulled on his winter gloves, and tugged at the lid. The sealer O-rings squeaked and then popped as he pulled the lid free. A desiccant pack lay on spools of Cordtex detonating cord that went down at least as far as the sunlight reached. He reattached the lid and opened the second ammo can. It was about half full of grenade hulls minus fuses.

While he reattached the lid of the second can, he became aware of a distant droning. He opened the third can more quickly. It was stacked with AR-15 assault rifle receivers—the business part of the gun, which normally bore the serial number. Maytubby lifted one out and turned it over. No serial. A blank receiver, untraceable. He screwed down the lid and reanchored the coveralls.

The drone grew louder. Without standing, he found the plane, a single-engine wing-over Cessna, approaching into a stout north wind. It was not going far beyond the field, because the southern half of Fort Sill was restricted airspace. He stood and managed a brisk nonchalance as he walked straight north, in the middle of the dirt strip, toward his pickup. The plane couldn't land without hitting him, and nobody shot through their own spinning prop. He took out his phone, switched it to selfie, and watched the plane descend behind him.

With his free hand, Maytubby took out his goober teeth and put them in. He watched the old Cessna slide east, off the glide path, and descend to maybe fifty feet as it approached him on the right. After photographing the plane, he spun in mock surprise, grinned, and waved like a thrilled child. The pilot wore a black hoodie and aviators. He didn't wave back. He did throttle up, loudly. Maytubby figured he would ascend until he could safely bank back toward the strip.

The Cessna's fuselage bore no tail number. It was as blank as the receivers. As the plane rose and pivoted, its wing top glared in the winter sun. Maytubby pocketed his phone and walked briskly, swinging his arms like a movie rube. Now, with a tailwind, the plane couldn't land. It buzzed past on his left. He again took out his cell, kept swinging his free arm, and watched over his shoulder as the Cessna banked left and descended. This time, though, it lined up on the dirt strip, and there was plenty of strip for a landing. Maytubby decided that running would instantly give him away and that in any case, he couldn't outrun the plane if it taxied off the strip and followed him into the rougher margins of the field.

The wheels chuffed when they struck the dirt, and the nose dipped as the pilot braked. The Cessna tacked slightly to the east as it approached Maytubby, who veered east himself to keep the prop between himself and the pilot. He pocketed his cell phone and waited until the plane was very close. As he expected, it pivoted on one braked wheel, and the fuselage came broadside to him. The parking brake clicked as the pilot's door flew open.

Maytubby spun and ran toward the feathering prop. The pilot bailed out of the plane, holding a pistol in his left hand while doing a bandy-legged dance around the wing struts and away from the prop. Maytubby leaned into his sprint as the pilot stepped sideways, raised his pistol, and fired. The round sang past Maytubby's head just as he dived to the left of the prop—keeping it in the pilot's line of fire—and rolled under the fuselage. He scrambled into the pilot's seat before the pilot could reverse course. He released the parking brake with his left hand, grabbed the throttle knob with his right. He barely nudged the throttle at first so the prop wouldn't suck up pebbles before it created a full wash. As the pilot made a run for the door, Maytubby plunged the throttle to the panel face. A volley of dust swept the man off balance. Maytubby applied left pedal so the elevator wouldn't hit him.

The Cessna thumped and lurched, shearing bluestem stalks as it covered the rough prairie between the strip and Maytubby's pickup. He throttled back so the plane wouldn't be lifted by the hard wind. Groping under the seats and in the door pockets, he came up with a mostly full box of 9mm Auto hollow-point cartridges and nothing else. No papers, no drugs. He emptied the ammo box out the window. Smears of dried adhesive showed him where the plane's registration plate had been peeled off.

A row of ruby digits glowed on the navigation radio—109.4, the frequency of the nearest beacon, Lawton-Fort Sill. Maytubby clicked through the preset frequencies. He recognized those he had flown to and from in planes with old avionics. He memorized the strangers.

Near the fence, Maytubby cut the prop, set the brake, and tossed the ignition key into the ditch. He flicked up the wire loop on the fence and—still obeying his father—closed the gate behind him. The pilot ran well—very well, considering the pistol—but he was still more than a quarter mile from his plane when Maytubby drove away from the mesquite thicket. At the first section-line stop sign, he saw in his mirror a Lilliputian figure with its legs spread. A tiny burst of smoke vanished on the wind. The nine struck the Ford's tailgate like a ball-peen hammer.

"Damn," he said.

CHAPTER 25

The young man Bond pulled over for speeding on US 177 west of
Mannsville had signed his ticket with a crude phallus. His cheeks were
tattooed with scorpions. When she tore the citation off her pad and
extended it to him, he gripped the steering wheel and glared straight
ahead. She dropped it in his lap. He snatched it up, wadded it in a ball,
and tossed it in the back seat.

She closed her citation holder and watched a scaup dunk between
the ice crusts on Wolf Creek. Scorpion Guy tried to peel out, but
his old Chevy Sonic stalled. Bond laid her citation holder on the
cruiser's windshield and stood until the gray-primered Sonic disappeared. High in the cold sky, horsetail cirrus clouds feathered south
in advance of a norther.

Bond heard the cycle's wail before it crested the creek riser. She
glanced at her radar display. It leapt from 0 to 86. As she reached
for the door handle, the bike's pitch fell to a growl; its speed plum-
meted. The cruiser's strobes still pulsed. Bond drew her hand back and
watched the yellow dirt bike coast almost silently around the cruiser
and stop on the shoulder. Its rider, wearing tan coveralls, a metallic

silver helmet, and black leather gloves, balanced the bike with his right leg and kicked down the stand with his left. He pulled off his helmet, set it on the tank, and shook out his hair. Richard James pulled off his gloves, laid them on the helmet, put his hands back on the handlebars so Bond could see them. Mr. Manners.

Bond set her palm on the butt of her old Smith and Wesson, dropped her index finger alongside the holster. She walked slowly toward James and stopped just behind him. Without moving his hands, he turned a broad smile and bright lapis eyes on her. She instinctively let her hand slip off the pistol, then instantly brought it back. A disarming character. And he hadn't said a word.

"Your license under your coveralls?" Bond said.

"Yes, Officer."

"You can get off and get it."

James held down his helmet and gloves while he dismounted. He faced Bond and unzipped his coveralls to below his waist. He was wearing a navy twill shirt, which looked ironed, and tight jeans. When he had jimmied his wallet out of his jeans, Bond stepped toward him to take his license with her left hand. She kept her right hand on the revolver. "My registration and insurance are in the left saddlebag."

Bond nodded once. "You can get 'em out." These she took with her left hand, also. "Now, sir, please zip up your coveralls and stand in front of your motorcycle, facing me."

Oklahoma had not adopted the federal Real ID standards for driver's licenses, so the one bearing James' photo alongside the name Francis Klaus was technically valid. The address was on Goad Road in Bray. Bond said, "Bray. Let's see. What's that school's mascot?"

"Donkey, ma'am," James said.

"Mmmm," she said. "I had a cousin lived close to this address on Goad."

James cocked his head and grinned. "It's a small world."

Bond retrieved the citation holder and began writing the ticket. "People call you Francis?"

More than a second passed before James said, "Frank."

Bond was looking at the last name on the license when he spoke. Somebody was lazy before they went into the DPS office. Klaus was an anagram of Sulak. She gave her citation pad the stink-eye as she copied all the bogus things. A box truck braked noisily as it topped the riser behind her. She saw the Sentinel logo and scowled as it passed. James' eyes never flinched.

"Rough day, Officer?"

Bond continued to write as she talked to her hand. "Yeah. I lost that cousin a couple of days ago." She looked up.

James pulled a frown and knitted his brow, looked into her eyes. "Oh, I'm sorry to hear that."

"She lived in that little white frame house at the intersection of Goad and Farmer's." James was good. He never broke eye contact. "Next section over from you. West. Propane tank in the front yard?"

If you stood in the middle of that intersection, you couldn't see a building for a mile in any direction.

James blinked but didn't fall for it.

Bond finished the citation, held it out to James with his documents. As his face came closer, Bond lifted the papers so he would raise his eyes. "Her name was Alice Lang."

This time, a fleeting squint, a brow tic. Not fear or anger, but skepticism. Bond got more than she angled for.

James quickly retrieved his solemnity. "I'm sorry. I didn't know the lady. I'm sure she was a fine Christian and is walking with her sweet Jesus through the green fields of paradise." His soul patch glistened.

Bond set cold eyes on him. "Only thing I'm sure of is, she's layin' on an autopsy table in Oklahoma City. A nine through her brain."

Folding his documents, James turned toward his bike. He stowed his registration and insurance in the saddlebag, faced Bond as he put away his billfold and zipped up his coveralls. "Manslayers and thieves. Defilers. Roaming this beautiful land like jackals." The visor fell across his face. He snapped on his gloves and slowly drove west.

After his silhouette had sunk under the near horizon, Bond studied the empty road.

CHAPTER 26

Maytubby had parked on a dirt road paralleling the makeshift airstrip, about half a mile away.

The aged Cessna buzzed into the air more than thirty minutes later. Either Lefty had emptied all the prepper barrels into the Cessna's seats, or Maytubby had pitched his keys too far. When Maytubby found the plane with his field glasses, it was banking east, toward his parking spot. It followed the military reservation boundary; flying low and slow, it passed just behind the pickup, then revved and made a turning climb to the southeast.

Laying the glasses on the seat, Maytubby picked up his phone and examined the list of navigation beacons he had made from the plane's avionics and a digital aeronautical chart. A string of them led west—one in Altus, Oklahoma; one near Amarillo, Texas; and two in New Mexico: Tucumcari and Moriarty. Another string went the plane's direction: Ardmore, Texoma—beacons he knew already—and Paris, Texas. He had driven through Paris but never flown there.

Maytubby switched from the list back to the aeronautical chart. A plane without tail numbers would attract attention at the Paris airport.

He counted seven smaller fields within fifteen miles. Who knew how many unidentified strips there were like the one he had discovered.

The Mooney Mustang, which had flown west toward Altus, still bore its tail number. Did that mean it landed at towered fields, such as Amarillo, where traffic controllers would see it? Maytubby entered the number in the FAA Aircraft Registry. It belonged to a 1970 Piper Cherokee owned by David Fisk of Rolla, Missouri. He then searched the FAA Accident and Incident Data. The Cherokee had crashed and burned on a stormy approach to a rural Arkansas airstrip years ago. Its owner had died in the crash. The plane had never been deregistered, so its number lived on.

Maytubby dismissed the FAA site and called Lighthorse Dispatch in Ada.

"Hey, Bill's cell."

"Hey, Sheila."

"You're in that old truck, without your gadgets."

"If things get hot, I have a flashing red light to stick on the roof."

"More fun than all the gadgets, after all. Where are you?"

"Comanche country."

"Want me to tell Chief Fox you drove the rustlers to ground?"

"I need something from NLETS, and even my gadgets won't get me that. Only you, Sheila."

"Must be some big-time rustlers. Hold on a sec while I log in." Some prairie-grass stems tumbled across his hood. "Okay. Shoot."

"Duncan Calls."

Maytubby heard her typing. She didn't ask about the spelling, because Calls was a Chickasaw name.

"You want dates and details?"

"Evil deeds and places is good."

"The big ones are Laramie, Wyo … Sorry. Laramie, assault and battery. Moriarty, New Mexico, armed robbery."

"Could you photograph his mug shot and send it to my cell?"

"Yessir."

"Could you see if Calls is a registered citizen of the Nation?" An orange Kubota utility tractor rolled by, its gloved driver hunched into hooded khaki coveralls. It kicked up sand that crackled against the pickup's fender.

"La-la-la-la-la … *la.* Duncan Calls. Looks like it. And this picture is clearer than the MLET mugs. Lemme get my cell out of my purse." Maytubby heard some rummaging, then a shutter sound. "On its way. You need anything else?"

"That's all. Thanks."

Maytubby opened the message from Sheila. There he was, the Santa Fe handyman, the Sentinel counterman. He was much younger in the photo. But the same thin nose, strong cheekbones, long upper lip. The photo made his skin look more orange than wheat.

Maytubby saved the picture, used a photo editor to give Calls a baseball cap and sunglasses. In the ballpark, but hard to tell without the cockeyed teeth.

* * *

Stopped at a light in Duncan, Maytubby watched fast-food sacks and cups skitter across State 7 onto Halliburton's industrial campus. *Like ghosts from an enchanter fleeing.* Saint John's had taught him Shelley's poetry. Dust from oilfield supply lots eddied around his pickup. Like dust.

Why was everyone suddenly left-handed?

He turned onto Bois D'Arc Avenue, which became Old State 7, a more nuanced path into the nation. More goats and donkeys, for one thing. More ancient pumpjacks for another.

And even better than a nuance—a wrinkle: the Sentinel box truck refueling at a Shamrock station in Velma. At the pump behind it, Richard James was filling his Suzuki. Maytubby slid on sunglasses, tugged down the bill of the camo OU cap, then made a U-turn and pulled up to the pump opposite the truck, on the same island. Lon Crum was pumping the gas.

Halfway out the pickup door, Maytubby saw that Crum held a lit cigarette at his side. Instead of opening the Ford's gas cap and stoking the vapor, Maytubby walked to the front of the pickup and popped the hood. He kept an eye on the cigarette as he pulled the dipstick.

"Drop that butt, you dumbass!" It was Rooster, in the Sentinel cab. Crum's head bobbed, the cigarette fell, and he ground it out with his foot.

James sucked air through his teeth and shook his head as he capped the cycle tank. He had laid his helmet on the driveway, against the kickstand so it wouldn't tumbleweed.

"Were you raised by ba*boons*?" Rooster bawled. Crum's head bobbed again.

Maytubby checked and rechecked the fluids. James stood by his bike, his arms folded, watching Crum remove the nozzle and replace the cap. Maytubby shut the hood, slowly fished for his wallet, slowly searched for his credit card. Just as he was inserting it in the pump, James walked toward Crum, who opened the Sentinel truck cab, retrieved and handed to James a blue gym-size duffel and what appeared to be a twenty-round box of Browning .30-06 rounds. Blindly pressing random numbers for his zip code, Maytubby watched the duffel and box change hands. James' hand did not register the half pound that twenty cartridges would weigh. There were no visible rifles in James' mobile home in Gene Autry, and anyway, toting a deer carcass on his bike would require some creative trussing.

Now the real zip code had to go in fast. James had dropped the cartridge box into something inside the duffel and was unzipping one of his saddlebags. How little gas could Maytubby pump without making someone look? If he'd paid cash in advance, one gallon. The card meant he had credit, so two. His tank was almost full.

In Oklahoma City, a 1965 Ford would have drawn stares. Not here.

Rifle ammo was always common as dirt in Oklahoma, but since the rise of gun culture it had gotten to be downright wholesome, a token of virtue and unity. Those guys in the truck passing out the ammo? They must be all right! Safer to put contraband in a cartridge box than in a box of Milk Duds.

As James picked up his helmet and tugged it on, Maytubby

imagined the first mile of every road out of Velma. He hadn't seen which directions Rooster and James had come from. Might not matter anyway.

The bike made a U-turn and buzzed east on new State 7. Maytubby looked away from it, then deliberately replaced the nozzle and his gas cap. He slid rather than jumped into the cab and drove away slowly. In his mirror, he saw the Sentinel truck pull out the opposite direction.

James didn't bolt away. The bike cruised at five over the limit. Pickups had to pass both Maytubby and, a half mile down the road, James. Why was he going so slow?

The road bent northeast to skirt the Arbuckles, passing through Tatums and Hennepin. Pumpjacks nodded among clusters of black Angus. Dead vines shrouding an abandoned school were coated with white quarry dust.

The Suzuki's taillight glowed, and James turned south on Dolese Road, which became Butterly Road after it passed the Dolese quarry on its winding ascent into rougher country. After Maytubby passed the quarry, he narrowed the tail. If the bike took one of the branching trails, the stout north wind would shear its dust, make it harder to locate.

In the middle distance, a file of white wind turbines towered above red cedar scrub, their massive blades wheeling. Maytubby had not driven Dolese Road since the twenty-story machines were erected, and they jostled his memory, made him briefly dizzy. As the bike climbed toward the low summit, it scattered a rafter of turkeys into the brush.

When the blade shadows began to flick across Butterly Road, the bike peeled off on a smaller track. Maytubby slowed almost to a stop and saw that the track ended just a few yards into the scrub, at an old prefab pine cabin with a smoking metal chimney. A ventilated generator shed, painted to resemble a tiny Georgian house, stood some yards from the cabin, and beside that a few cords of neatly stacked oak firewood. Parked beside the firewood, facing the road, was a polished black 1991 Jeep Cherokee Laredo. No front tag, so likely an Oklahoma plate. He followed Butterly Road to the base of a turbine, made a three-point turn, turned off the Ford, and looked down toward the cabin. It was hidden by trees. He waited, listening to the blades scythe the air.

The cabin had no electrical service cable, no satellite dish, no propane tank. A generator that would fit in the small ventilated shed would go through twenty gallons of gas a day. There was no large gas tank in the yard, so that generator was not going to keep the peas frozen. It was for occasional use.

Ten minutes later, he started the pickup and descended the hill. In the second pass by the cabin he noticed that the clothesline poles were not connected and that the windows were dressed with white miniblinds, all of them closed.

No tokens of domesticity or vacation at the cabin. No flower pots, no floral thermometer, no chairs on the full-length porch, no dog, no tool shed. Nothing. He slowed for a truck leaving the quarry. Not even junk. Conspicuously junk-free, in fact. And who in Garvin County owned a ventilated generator shed disguised as a Georgian playhouse?

The Butterly cabin was the opposite of the Powell Road compound. It was itinerant lodging. But you noticed its austerity from the road. Not a good quality in a hideout. As Hannah would say, the cabin was a "stick-out" place.

The fastidious characters were Richard James and the tall fake casino guard. James lived in a mobile home in Gene Autry. The cabin seemed more like a place he would live. There was a chance he maintained it.

If James stayed a long time, he might be hooking up, in which case the duffel might be going someplace else. If he left quickly, he was delivering for the Sentinel crew.

Just beyond the quarry, Maytubby checked for trucks, stopped, and backed into an unfenced gap between two red cedars. The Suzuki passed a few minutes later. James did not turn his head. Maytubby waited for him to get on the highway before returning to the cabin. Whoever was inside had not likely seen the Ford.

The satellite view on Maytubby's cell showed a jeep trail descending from the turbines and looping a couple hundred yards behind the cabin. The north wind whipped his dust away from the cabin, so he nosed into some scrub oaks close to it. His binoculars showed him a turquoise New Mexico plate and a dealer sticker with the name Brewster in large type over a tiny, unreadable location. He searched the plate number on his cell, through a state site. It didn't belong to Duncan Calls, who would recognize him. Roger Teague. His address was in Moriarty. Didn't mean Duncan Calls wasn't in the cabin.

Maytubby fitted his gag teeth, mussed his hair, and donned his camo OU ball cap. The pilot was long gone. He walked from his truck to the back door of the cabin. A mechanical keypad lock was more evidence that people passed through this place. It was cheap, which meant that nothing valuable was stored here. He knocked politely. Some seconds passed. He banged.

The man who cracked the door was a lean stranger of middle height, balding, with a fifty-dollar haircut and manicured nails. He wore contacts on appraising garnet eyes. "How may I help you, sir?" Maytubby looked through the crack and saw the blue duffel beneath a kitchen table. The cabin was lit by skylights. Under oak smoke, he caught a whiff of male dorm room, though he saw no boy.

"I'm lost, man," Maytubby said. "I come up from Woodford, north of Fifty-Three, over the trails, to take a buddy to work at one of them new windmills. Now I can't find my way back to Seven from here. He give me bad directions. Can you help me?"

The man opened the door, came outside, and closed the door behind him. He pulled the doorknob with his left hand, but then, the knob was on his left. He wore ecru jeans and a tartan flannel shirt. Both were ironed, the jeans with a crease. "Certainly." He turned to face east. "Come right around to the big road in front of this cabin." He nodded toward the road. "Follow it north. You'll strike Seven in a few miles." He never pointed.

Maytubby gaped and shook his head. "You're my man." He jabbed an index finger in the air, spun it, and made to walk away. Then he stopped, turned, and said, "You got a beer for a vet?" Maytubby wasn't a vet.

The man said, "I don't drink. But if I did, sir, I'd give you one.

Thank you for your service." He turned, went inside, and shut the door.

"Certainly?" Creased ecru jeans? Worn by a native of Moriarty? A ventilated generator shed made to look like a Georgian house? Maytubby felt as if he'd walked out of Dusty Knob into a Wes Anderson movie.

He had added another fussy character to the roll. A few men in the Ada aristocracy sported the prep, but it was more common among Dallasites who owned the bigger vacation homes near Lake of the Arbuckles. This was not a vacation home.

Maytubby revved the Ford so the lodger could hear, then drove slowly down Butterly Road, past the cabin, so the lodger could see. The satellite photo on his phone showed only one trail ahead of him looping back up to the turbines. He took it.

After parking the Ford, removing his fake teeth, and straightening his hair, he took his binoculars and walked a quarter mile toward the back of the cabin. He knelt behind a large limestone rock, braced his elbows on it, and summoned patience for hours of nothing.

He had not gotten the glasses focused when the back door opened and the balding man appeared, wearing a navy Harrington jacket and carrying the blue duffel in his left hand. He pulled the door shut with his right. Handedness solved. Maytubby waited for the sound of the Jeep's ignition and then ran to his pickup.

After the Jeep passed in front of him on Butterly Road, Maytubby waited before pulling out. The balding man, who wasn't from around there, had surely bookmarked the antique Ford. State 7, where Butterly intersected it, had long sight lines in both directions, and the day was bright and clear.

Before he could reach the highway, two loaded trucks upshifted from the quarry road onto Butterly just ahead of him. By the time he hit State 7, the Jeep was over one of its horizons. Maytubby turned east toward home, passed the two quarry trucks, and phoned Dispatch.

"Hey, Bill."

"Hey, Sheila. Lost track of a black 1991 Jeep Cherokee Laredo with New Mexico plates." He waited for her to jot.

"Plates turquoise or gold?"

"Turquoise. Going east or west from Butterly on Seven. Not pursuing. Just like to know where he's going."

"I'll alert Eph, Katz, and the FBI."

"You're a mind reader, Sheila."

"Right. Just Lighthorse and Hannah?"

"Yes."

"Keeping your powder dry."

"One of my mottoes."

Maytubby heard Sheila calling the other cars. She came back to him. "I thought you could only have one motto. Like the Texas Rangers have 'One riot, one Ranger.'"

"See? They have another one. 'Courage, integrity, perseverance.'" Maytubby passed under I-35, crossed the Washita, and turned south on old US 77.

"That's a bunch of nothin'."

CHAPTER 27

Maytubby was negotiating the last hairpin curve before the Turner Falls overlook when the Jeep appeared below him on his right, climbing toward him. Must have overshot the dogleg turnoff in Davis. Or was he flipping the tail?

Maytubby gained the hill's summit, turned into the overlook lot, and parked behind a bank of pay telescopes. The Jeep also pulled into the lot but did not follow Maytubby. In his rearview mirror, Maytubby saw the balding man talking on his cell, looking up the highway. There were cell antennas atop the shuttered souvenir shop.

A guy who had taken his pal to work on a wind turbine was not a tourist, so Maytubby stayed in his pickup and phoned Sheila.

"So what's another one of your mottoes?"

"'Convincingly vigilant.'"

The line was quiet a second. "I don't know about you, Sergeant."

"That black Jeep is parked across from me at the Turner Falls overlook. It was behind me coming up the switchbacks."

"Hold on." He waited while she canceled the request. "Jeep doesn't know you're a cop. Does he know you were tailing him before he started tailing you?"

"I don't think he's tailing me. If he leaves before I do, I can go back to tailing him."

"How do the falls look?"

"A little ice on the edges of the fan."

"Did you know Turner's first name was Mazeppa? Hold on." Maytubby heard Sheila's radio, then her voice. The balding man was texting now. "Isn't that a weird name?"

Maytubby knew that Turner was a Scot named for a Cossack made famous by Lord Byron. And that he married a Chickasaw woman named Laura Johnson. "That is a very weird name," he said.

The falls were louder than the wind. In his mirror, the Jeep's brake light went off. The balding man put down his phone as he pulled onto 77 going south. "Jeep's southbound, Sheila."

"Do-si-do."

"And away we go." They hung up. He gave the Jeep thirty seconds, watched it top the next rise before he pulled out of the lot. The road bisected long chains of limestone slabs that leaned like Puritan tombstones. A wildfire had left nothing but tree carcasses in the graveyard.

The Jeep bypassed Ardmore, headed east on US 177 toward Tishomingo. The balding man had no need to go to Sentinel. Unlike Richard James, this guy was making time: he slowed a bit for the little towns but kept at eighty-five between. Not enough traffic for people to report cops on their phone apps. One of the Jeep's brake lights was out.

A few miles before Mannsville, Maytubby saw the brake light flash as the Laredo topped a rise. When Maytubby came over the same hill, he had to hit his brakes to avoid a sheriff's cruiser in mid U-turn. Under the strobes, he recognized Bond, who appeared to be eating with her right hand while she steered with her left. From their CLEET days, he recalled her nonchalance in pursuit.

The Jeep was already out of sight, and the cruiser soon was, too. Maytubby parked on the shoulder and watched a scaup on Wolf Creek. He would stay put for as long as he judged it would take Bond to pull the Jeep over and get the balding man fishing for his wallet. Then he would pass them and lie low in Mannsville. Bond knew that Maytubby was interested in the Jeep. The balding fellow had stepped on a crack.

* * *

The Laredo driver pulled over quickly and was dangling his documents out the window before Bond told Tish what she was doing and got his tag up on her screen. Trying to rush her. As she walked slowly toward the Jeep, the driver lifted something into the back seat with his right hand. Then he tilted his rearview mirror down and fingered something on the dash. She stood close behind the Jeep a long time, noting the fine white dust in the weather-stripping joints, a trailer hitch, some scratches that had been touched up. No decals, but a dealer sticker: Brewster Jeep in Paris, Texas. The cargo floor mat and spare cover shone with spray tire polish.

For a middle-aged vehicle, the upholstery in the back seat looked new. What the driver had thrown back there was a blue duffel. Its drape suggested something rigid inside, maybe a box. As Bond approached the driver and stopped just behind him, he raised the documents and bent his arm backward toward her. She didn't take them but stood still, in the driver's blind spot, pretending to write on her citation pad while she looked over the dash and front seat.

A radar detector was mounted on the passenger's visor. The burned-out brake light was a piece of luck. A cell phone rested in a vent-mounted cradle just to the right of the driver, its screen dark. This must have been what the driver touched. Paper maps were harder to hide. Too bad they were a thing of the past.

Bond moved a little nearer the driver but did not yet bend toward him. He twisted his head back and then tilted it up and up, straining to find her face. Fancy haircut, manicured nails, new dark-blue jacket. Ironed jeans that weren't even jeans color. A dude. He probably bought French soap on the internet.

She suddenly dropped her face very near his, leaving his hand, with its documents, waving above her head. She wanted him to see her look at the duffel over his shoulder. His eyes went to the rearview mirror.

"License-registration-insurance," she said. He frowned and pivoted to bring them down without touching her. She didn't oblige but waited until he had gotten them inside the car and then back into her hand. She clipped them on her citation holder. When she looked up, he was looking at the bag in the mirror. He didn't ask why he was being stopped.

Back in her cruiser, Bond ran Roger Teague's New Mexico plate and DL. Nothing. But New Mexico had not adopted the Real ID, either. She called Maytubby's cell.

"Hannah. Did I see you eating while making a U-turn?"

"Lunchtime. You parked just over the hill."

"Yes. My vehicle is artfully concealed."

"You cover it with dead branches like they taught us in policeman school?" Hannah deadpanned.

"It's a good thing civilians aren't privy to our stratagems."

"Nnnnhh. So why are you following Roger Teague?"

"I was following Richard James. He was carrying a blue duffel and something in a cartridge box to a cabin by Hennepin. Teague was staying there. It's off the grid. I think it may be a …"

"Wait, he's moving the duffel."

"And now you've got cause."

"That I do."

"I'll move to the top of the hill and back you up. He won't see me, because of the sticks."

"Tell you when I'm done with him."

She put her phone away and completed the citation. Teague's address was in Moriarty, New Mexico. For some reason, the name looked suspicious.

When she handed Teague the aluminum citation holder with his documents and a pen clipped to the top, she kept her palm on the butt of her pistol. "You can take your license and papers after you sign. Keep the pink copy of the citation." He did as he was told, handed the holder to her. She snugged it between her duty belt and her spine.

She stood, impassive, while Teague stowed all his documents. He looked up at her blankly.

"Where is the duffel that was on the back seat when I stopped you?"

He blinked.

Then he said, "It's on the floor behind me. It's a deer rifle."

"Which half?"

"It's broken down."

"Deer season's over."

He shook his head. "I don't hunt."

"I was gonna say. You're some boots and a orange hat short of an outfit."

"I'm taking it to an acquaintance."

Bond stepped back and said, "Sir, please step out of your vehicle."

When she had frisked Teague, walked him to the bar ditch, and instructed him to sit there, Bond pulled on vinyl gloves from her duty belt and unzipped the blue bag on the Jeep's roof. When Teague was looking the other way, she also pulled her phone out of her pants pocket. The duffel was deep enough to hide her hands and the phone from Teague.

Inside, packed with squares of cardboard, she found the disassembled deer rifle. Except it was an AR-15 assault-style rifle. And bump-stock hardware that would legally turn the semiautomatic rifle into a machine gun. There was no serial number on the receiver. Two empty thirty-round magazines lay on the hard bottom of the duffel, beside a .30-06 cartridge box. Bond opened it and found a smaller, white box. Crude black type on the box said the contents were hollow-point .223 Remington cartridges. Beyond the ammo description, there was no other print on the box—no trademark or address. She pulled out its plastic tray and found only thirty-five rounds in the fifty slots. She photographed everything with her phone.

She looked at Teague, who wore only a jacket against the cold. He flicked his eyes away and dug his hands deeper into his pockets.

All the bag's contents back in place, Bond zipped it closed. She stopped and shook her head. Then she reopened the bag and turned over the .30-06 box. On the bottom, in faint pencil, Bond read "137007 County Road 64783 Paris."

"Stupid," she whispered to herself.

She photographed the address and messaged it and the other photos to Maytubby.

"You can get up," she said to Teague. She handed him the duffel. "You're good to go." He took it and walked in front of her to the Jeep. When he had shut the door, Bond leaned down and said, "Deer rifle. That thing is gonna spew lead all over the ranch. I hope your friend knows how to field-dress a steer." He nodded slowly. "Drive safely."

"I will, Officer."

After he had gone down the road, Bond called Maytubby. "I've got 'im, Hannah."

"He called that mess a deer rifle."

Maytubby crossed Turkey Creek, its banks creased with sleet. The Jeep was a half mile ahead, going the speed limit.

"See?" Maytubby said to Bond. "Even with the blank receiver, if he'd just claimed the gun and bragged about how badass he'd made it."

"Doesn't know the ways."

Where Oklahoma 1 veered north to Tishomingo, the Jeep went south on US 177 and then stair-stepped southeast toward the Red River. It passed into the Choctaw Nation, where Maytubby was cross-deputized, then crossed the Red River into Texas, where he wasn't. Before it reached the outlying acreages of Paris on US 271, the Jeep turned west just where Maytubby's phone said it should. Maytubby paused a few seconds at the intersection because other traffic on a back road was more interesting than it was on a busy highway. He watched steam draft off the distant towers of the Campbell's Soup cannery.

County Road 64783 wound through the buckskin grass and compact thickets of the Post Oak Savannah. Open hay barns were down to half their winter store. A rancher surrounded by red Brangus swung a pickax to break ice in a galvanized livestock tank.

The road swerved sharply to the right and plunged into a shadowed alley of post oak and red cedar. A mile passed before Maytubby reached a creek bridge, its rusted guardrails splayed. A sounder of feral hogs moved down the stream bank, rooting in the leaves.

As the destination approached, Maytubby slowed until he saw the Jeep, its brake light glowing, about a thousand yards ahead. He slowed, set his cell camera to full-zoom video, and held it against the driver's-side window. Then he drove just over a conspicuously slow speed toward the black Jeep. He could see it turn left into a drive, where two figures met it.

When he got closer, he saw that the figures were men in military fatigues, with assault-style rifles slung over their shoulders. They wore fatigue hats blazoned with an image he couldn't make out. In case his camera was poorly aimed, he briefly moved his eyes to the Jeep just before he passed it. Teague was handing the duffel to one of the musketeers. There was a single flag atop each tall gatepost. One was the Confederate battle flag. The other he couldn't recognize. It wasn't burnt orange, so probably not a Longhorns flag.

The jeep backed onto the road about a half mile behind Maytubby, then headed back the way it came. Maytubby pulled over, found on his phone another back road that returned him to US 271 north of where Teague would join it. But he had more distance to cover, so he had to speed.

Parked behind a bait stand named Stinky's, Maytubby watched 271 and his video. The logos on the caps and the second flag matched—a hand lifting a torch. It reminded Maytubby of Jean-Jacques Rousseau's tomb in the other Paris—the philosopher's sculpted hand poking the torch of liberty through the wall of his tomb.

He looked down the highway toward Paris. The most famous tombstone there was a statue of Jesus wearing cowboy boots.

When Teague handed over the duffel, he had taken something from the man's hand—maybe an envelope. That might explain why Teague duplicated the Cessna's delivery route—if the Cessna did indeed fly to Paris. Also, there had been no bump stocks in the prepper cans. Maybe a gun considered truly badass got its own courier.

Maytubby paused his video, looking at the musketeers' goateed faces. He shrugged and started to click off the phone when it chimed for a text. Nichole Hewitt had written to Jill and him: *Still shaky. Will let you both know when I feel up to talking. Mom is doing a great job with the girls.* He clicked the screen black.

The Jeep shot past and was almost to the Red River before Maytubby picked it up. Near the Choctaw Casino in Grant, the brake light glowed a few hundred yards before the Jeep passed a parked trooper. Teague did not turn west in Grant and retrace his route but continued north to the Indian Nation Turnpike. At Antlers, he exited at State 3, following the Muddy Boggy past Iron Stob Road and Atoka into the old mining town of Coalgate, where he pulled into the gravel parking lot of Lorenza Mercante's liquor store on South Broadway.

Maytubby watched the store through the window of a Grab-n-Go while he paid for a bag of roasted peanuts. Teague emerged with two paper sacks, which he set on the floor of the Jeep's back seat. After he had driven away, Maytubby parked in his place and watched as the Jeep turned into an auto parts store farther up Broadway. Taillight. Maytubby took off his cap and bounded into the store.

Lorenza Mercante looked up when the door buzzed. She sat on a stool in the afternoon light, her expression pleasantly neutral as he walked quickly to the back of the store. Then she beamed, and her eyes widened and shone. "I didn't recognize you with your clothes on." She shook her head and fake coughed. "Not your uniform. You know. I mean."

"*Mufti,*" he said. "Old Chickasaw term."

"You're pulling my leg." She leaned toward him, squeezed his forearm, and stage-whispered as she pointed to the door, "That guy one of your desperadoes?"

"I don't know, Ms. Mercante. I am following him. Can you tell me what he bought?"

"Lorenza. Same thing he bought a month or so ago: two bottles of Blanton's Single Barrel, with the little jockey on top." She tapped an imaginary jockey, then ran her fingers through her coffee hair. "He pulled a stack of hundreds out of an envelope and thumbed one to me."

"Anything written on the envelope?"

She stared at the counter and frowned. "I couldn't see the front of it." Then she looked up. "He doesn't wear a ring. So he irons creases in his jeans. Or pays somebody to." She looked at the legs of Maytubby's jeans.

"Don't worry," he said.

"After I sacked his Bourbons, he folded the top of each sack three times and then creased it with his fingers." She bounced an index finger on her temple. "*Pazzo.*" Crazy. Lorenza Mercante was descended from Italian coal-mining families that had worked the Coalgate and Lehigh seams long ago.

"If you think of …"

"You're still in my contacts, from the time I spied on the roughneck for you."

"I really appreciate it, Mm … Lorenza."

"There we go. Like I said before, nice airstrip right behind the store."

He looked over her shoulder and through the back window. Coalgate Municipal's orange wind sock was stiff with the north breeze. "Right." He nodded and smiled. "Thanks again."

The Jeep was turning onto Broadway when Maytubby left the store. Teague turned left on Ohio, which turned into Oklahoma 31. Maytubby had never told Lorenza Mercante he was engaged. He seldom saw her. He also left her out of his conversations with Jill Milton. He didn't know whether these facts were important.

Dropping south on State 48 at Clarita, Teague braked and then passed an enclosed Amish buggy. As Maytubby approached, its turn light flashed, and it wheeled onto Shellpit Road. The snowy-bearded driver wore a black watch cap.

Teague turned onto Bromide Road, which threaded the limestone ruin of Bromide's mineral springs resort. Then he went full rural on unpaved Coatsworth Road. For a New Mexican, he knew him some Johnston County Roads.

Maytubby had to hang far back now. The road was deserted, the sight lines long. Teague passed Witch Hole and Houghtubby Spring, headed for Blue River. Maytubby reckoned that this back road trek would eventually get Teague to Powell Road or James' mobile home.

But then the Laredo jagged north on Deadman Springs Road.

Now to see who got the next bottle of hooch.

Forested knobs cast long shadows across dun grassland and silty green ponds. Just beyond the road's dogleg west, the Jeep, almost a mile ahead of him, disappeared. Maytubby stopped and glassed the road ahead. Nothing but two turkey buzzards wheeling over the plain of the Blue. He looked up the satellite map of the land ahead. It was a summer photo. The knolls gave way to low, timbered hogbacks. A feeble trail left the road at the dogleg and vanished under the canopy. Except for a couple of deer stands, there were no visible driveways or structures for miles to the northeast.

As Maytubby neared the road less traveled, he saw a padlocked steel livestock gate. Atop one of its stanchions perched two wireless security cameras, one of them trained on Deadman Springs Road. He stayed on the road through the dogleg and drove across the Blue to Connerville.

From the parking lot behind the Chickasaw Nation Senior Center, he phoned Hannah Bond, who was off shift. "Where did Mr. Deer Rifle get to?" she said. He heard a train horn on her end.

"White supremacists' camp north of Paris. He's back in Oklahoma."

"His license didn't say corrective lenses, but if he didn't catch on to that old Ford in two hundred miles, he needs 'em."

"Who did see me in the Ford was a pilot for this bunch. Flies out of a dirt strip in Cache. He shot my tailgate with a pistol from four hundred yards."

"The Ford would make a bigger impression than goober teeth."

"The master race paid Teague a stack of Franklins for the rifle. He used some of it to buy two bottles of that posh Bourbon James had on his counter. Had to leave him up in the hogbacks above Deadman Springs Road. Gate. Cameras. You watching the James estate?"

"Found a back way in off Redbud Lane. Steiners doing the rest of the walking."

"I would need a spotter to lift those things."

A compact sedan drove into the parking lot. Maytubby watched a man his own age lift two young girls, clearly his children, out of car seats and walk them to the senior center.

"Spavined Bronco at the single-wide. Tall tanks in the back. That rifle and bump stock were not worth a stack of Franklins. Maybe the blank receiver."

The father held open the door for his girls, who walked solemnly in.

"Bill, you there?"

"Sorry. Say again."

"At James' trailer. A crapped-out blue-green Bronco with tanks in the bed."

"Welder from out by Lone Grove. The casino thieves, likely including the guy who killed Tommy Hewitt, burned their fake uniforms in his shop. In a barrel. Another pickup came later, and the driver dumped the ashes in Caddo Creek."

"Some greenhorn Assistant US attorney'll be waving fly zippers in the jury's faces. Wonderin' if she took a bum turn in life."

The Laredo turned onto US 377. It passed the senior center and turned west.

"Here's Teague."

"No flies on Ironed Man."

"Headed west on Spring Creek Road." Maytubby cranked up the Ford.

"You'll see whether he stops at Powell Road before he gets here."

"Yeah, but I won't know why."

"Those goobers don't even get some whiskey. Later."

There was only one way west over this stretch of the Rock Prairie—one bridge over Pennington Creek. Maytubby could straggle. In the distance, the Laredo threw a scud of yellow dust across the low, cold sun.

When the Mill Creek water tank appeared, Maytubby remembered that the route to Powell Road passed the Hewitts' home. He slowed to let Teague negotiate the village. Behind a front-yard fence, two motionless sorrel horses gazed southward.

Thumping over the quarry train tracks, Maytubby saw, beyond the Hewitts' bare pecans, Nichole's mother bundling her grandchildren out of her car. Nichole was not in the car. Maytubby turned his eyes to Daube Ranch Road.

Climbing out of the thicket of Bee Branch, the road wound between dolomite outcrops as it skirted a quarry. It swung into darkening swales of grassland. When Teague turned onto Powell Road, Maytubby gave him an even longer lead.

In deep twilight, Maytubby watched from the knob east of the compound as the guard's blue Dakota pickup pulled aside to admit the Jeep. The pickup followed Teague back to the compound. Hannah would tell Maytubby if Teague joined the welder and James in Gene Autry.

CHAPTER 28

As Maytubby climbed the stairs to Jill Milton's garage apartment, he could hear her frailing the mountain minor chords of "Shady Grove." When he came through the door, she looked up from the couch, frowning. She played a little softer.

"It's our soundtrack these days," he said.

She nodded. "The road *is* dark." At the end of the chorus, the drone G lingered as she set the old Deering in its cradle.

Maytubby sat beside her. He spread his hand over her back and pulled her toward him. "What's in the oven, sweet potatoes?"

"I love it when you talk dirty." She kissed him. "Butternut squash from the nation's garden last fall. I'm giving it a little head start on the stuffing. You smell like oak smoke and cigarette smoke."

"Since it's so close to dinner, I'll say only that a certain person was smoking at the gas pump next to mine."

"Why don't you just lie and spare me pain?"

"I didn't want to raise suspicion."

"Like about a smoking girlfriend with a fireplace?" She narrowed her eyes.

"For example."

"Hah."

"See how it sounds: 'There was this guy smoking …'"

She gave him the fake side-eye when she rose.

Maytubby scanned ramekins on the kitchen counter. "Ah, the tony stuffing. You find crystallized ginger at DK's?"

"Yes, and you see those are native pecans. I saw them in my head-lights leaving Nichole's."

"I know they're sweeter than papershells, but we're gonna need the big hammer."

"You can start on that," she said, nodding at the pecans and taking a sweating bottle of white wine and some peach salsa out of the refrig-erator. She set the salsa on the counter. With her free hand, she tapped on her laptop. Café Noir's cover of a Stravinsky andante began quietly.

Maytubby stood and walked to the counter. Jill Milton set a wine-glass in front of him. He held up a hinged lever nutcracker from early in the past century. "Really? This job calls for a bench vise. Do you have a bench vise?"

She set out the salsa and a few chips, poured wine into his glass.

He canted his head to read the bottle's label. "Our own Waddell's Vineyard bottles a wine I've never heard of?"

"Viognier. It pairs with butternut squash."

"And you would know that how?"

"I waited tables in Brooklyn. You knew that." She filled her own glass.

"Yeah, I just imagined …"

"Vegan enchiladas and the house red?" She raised her eyebrows.

"Yeah, like that." He fitted a pecan in the cracker's jaws and faked a grimace as he squeezed the handles. The nut snapped loudly. Pieces of shell ricocheted off their glasses. "Got-dang!" He dropped the nut into his palm and took a metal pick to its meat. "When you were waiting tables, is that when you were seeing the fire-eater dude from Texar-kana? What was his name?"

"'Dude.' When are you going to let the mists of the past shroud him forever?"

Maytubby cracked another pecan and said, "Never!"

They dipped chips in the peach salsa. Jill melted butter in a copper skillet and sautéed shallots over low heat. Maytubby chopped the pecans and some shelled walnuts, dried cranberries, yellow raisins, and crystallized ginger. He fed Jill a piece of the ginger with his fingers. "My knife is really gummy," he said. He slid a pan of nutmeats into the toaster oven. "I think Waddell's regional label should be Clear Boggy Valley." He held his glass up to the light. "A crisp, peachy Oklahoma Viognier with notes of soybean and methane."

She took the squash halves out of the oven and set the pan behind the skillet. "Speaking of smoking at a gas pump, I also saw Slob today. In Comanche. He was with Rooster."

Maytubby took his eyes off the toaster oven and looked at her.

"Rooster didn't see me. He was in the Sentinel truck, smoking and texting." She picked up a wooden spatula, tilted the skillet, and pushed the shallots into a small bowl. "I saw the other guy on his knees, stocking a machine down a hall. *De*tour. When I was in an empty classroom talking with a health teacher about the Eagle play, she saw Rooster through a window, sitting in the truck. Then she closed the blinds and hugged herself."

Maytubby turned off the toaster oven and slid out the pan of nuts. "The horror?"

"Yeah. But not just his looks. Last weekend, her family was walking through a parking lot in Ardmore? Rooster drove up, jumped out of his pickup with a pistol, and accused her husband of cutting him off. Shouted obscenities, waved the gun around. Made the kids cry. Got back in his pickup and peeled out of the lot."

Maytubby shook the roasted nuts into the skillet. "Did ..."

"I told the teacher my fiancé's a cop. White late-model Ford Supercab, big front bumper."

"The Supercab that passed you the morning you were on your way to Gonzalez's—white Ford?"

Jill knitted her brow, stirred the skillet, and turned off the fire. "Ford, yeah. Light. Silver or white."

"This investigation is lousy with white Ford Supercabs. But there wasn't one parked at Rooster's workplace—Sentinel Vending—when I was there."

She spooned the stuffing into the squash hearts. "Maybe they like to share."

"I had never thought of that." Maytubby opened a cabinet and took out a square green bottle of olive oil and small bags of spices. He set them on the counter. "I was out your way this morning. Cache."

"Home of Quanah Parker's White Star House."

"Yes. And of a makeshift landing strip with buried contraband. And a dubious Cessna that buzzed the Ford."

"Wait," Jill said. "What …"

"*Here's* a strange," Maytubby said quickly. "The counter guy at Sentinel was my landlord's handyman when I lived in Santa Fe. Small-time crook. My landlord died, but his daughter told me today the guy's name is Duncan Calls."

Jill took a sip of the Viognier and looked at Maytubby. "Lots of Callses on the Dawes rolls."

"And Duncan Calls is a Chickasaw citizen."

"Did he recognize you?"

"Don't think so." Maytubby drizzled the squash halves with olive oil and seasoned them lightly with cardamom, nutmeg, and cinnamon. He crumbled brown sugar over everything and slid the pan back in the oven.

They stood near the small white range because it was warmer there. Jill said, "I got Nichole's text in Comanche."

"I was in suburban Paris."

"It reminded me that her mother lost her own father when she was young, like you lost your mom. She might be an insightful guide."

"I was passing through Mill Creek late this afternoon and saw her taking the girls out of her car. Nichole wasn't with them."

"I hope the FBI leaves her in peace." Jill sipped her wine. "Why were you in the City of Lights?"

"I was watching a fastidious man from Moriarty deliver an illegal rifle to a white-supremacist camp in the country. The Marietta embezzler picked up the duffel holding the rifle from Rooster and the Stank at the aforementioned gas station. After the Moriarty guy received the bag, Hannah knew I was tailing him, so she stopped him for a taillight. He acted weird about the bag, so she had cause to look inside."

"And she didn't arrest him, because then he wouldn't lead you to his clients."

Maytubby nodded.

"And how do you know he's fastidious?"

"His ecru jeans are creased." He did not mention the liquor sack creases.

"Where did he go?"

"To the Powell Road compound. Hannah is watching the embezzler's mobile home. Shady gathering. The fastidious man may show up there later."

"Get the place cleaned up."

Maytubby sipped his wine, picked up a stray pecan chip and ate it. "Actually, the embezzler—his name is Richard James—keeps a tidy trailer. Also trims his soul patch."

"Dude wore a soul patch."

"Another reason to distrust the embezzler. Also, you lie like a rug."

Jill set her wineglass on the counter, took Maytubby's and did the same. She took his hand and led him into her bedroom. "Let's burn the squash."

CHAPTER 29

When Maytubby's cell vibrated, he was washing the last bit of pecan charcoal off a dinner dish. The shower spattered in the back.

Hannah said, "Where'd he buy a new bulb for the Jeep?"

"Coalgate. Hooch, too. He bring that with him?"

"He brought something small. But it's dark and the moon's not doing me much good. For some reason, they didn't leave the blinds open so I could see their every move."

Maytubby set the dish in the drainer. He listened while Hannah breathed.

"You know what?" she said. "This watching people through binoculars at night is bullshit. I'm going to Alice's house. Eph told me the OSBI car was there today."

"I won't tell Scrooby you're horning in."

"He's got a cadet working down here. I think it's past her bedtime."

* * *

On the way to Wapanucka, Bond stopped at her house in Tishomingo. In her bathroom, she opened the cupboard door, pulled out all the folded towels, and tucked them under her arm. In the bedroom, she stripped the blankets off the single bed and draped them over her neck. From her single dresser, she grabbed a set of long underwear, which she pinched under her chin. With her free arm, she retrieved a magnifying glass from her rat drawer and stuck it in her hip pocket. She grabbed a fistful of Slim Jims from a kitchen drawer and stuck them in her back pocket with the glass, microwaved a mug of cold coffee, and set it on the Buick's hood while she stowed everything else in the trunk.

* * *

Now there was yellow crime scene tape around Alice Lang's dark house, strung between arborvitae trees. Bond doused her headlights, pulled disposable gloves and evidence bags from the door pocket, and slid the elastic band of a Petzl lamp over her head. Her duty belt, cell phone, aviator hat, and pistol lay in the Buick's passenger seat.

She ducked under the tape, slipped on the gloves, and opened the fuse box. The spare key was gone.

She closed the box and stared at its cover while she brought to mind the inside of each of the house's old sash windows. She focused on their sweep locks—always visible because Alice loved sunlight and kept the blinds open. Going from room to room in her mind's eye, Bond remembered which windows Alice opened in temperate weather. Then she tried to remember whether any of those had broken or missing locks. A flock of resident Canada geese honked by, low in the sky.

The middle window in the living room. It was missing the sweep altogether. With her Petzl, she found a cinder block to stand on, giving her better leverage to thumb the sash bars up. After she got the window open, she had to push past the closed blinds with her head. The blinds scraped off her headlamp as she hand-walked her legs in.

The house no longer smelled of boy, anise, sage, and oak smoke as it had just after Alice was killed. The scents more familiar to Bond had returned: stale mercaptan, dryer sheets, and Pine-Sol.

Bond picked up the headlamp and held it in her right hand. She wasn't hiding the light; the wall of evergreens outside did that, at least on the back and two sides. She was here to crawl the wooden floor and glean.

As she lay prone, Bond took the magnifying glass from her back pocket. Breathing as shallowly as she could, smelling a faint blend of paste wax and Pine-Sol, she moved the glass slowly, the enlarged area lit by her lamp, which she shined at an angle to the floor. Her peripheral vision was blackness.

If the cadet wore shoe covers and didn't do what Bond was doing now, there would be little on the floor unrelated to the crime. Alice Lang swept, washed, waxed, and buffed her oak floor obsessively. The cadet would have spotted anything as obvious as a dusty footprint.

Whoever took Alice had also closed the blinds, probably before she arrived. Bond first crawled along the baseboard under the windows. When she came to furniture, she stood and examined its surfaces. After finishing the baseboard perimeter, she crawled one length of the living room, exhausting a yard-wide strip, then pivoted and worked her way back on the next parallel strip. She found four days' dust blown through fissures in the sashes, a couple of mouse turds, a flake of dried leaf.

In the dark kitchen, a wall clock ticked off the seconds until dawn. When she had covered half the floor, she looked at her watch. Two hours and ten minutes had passed since she left the Buick. Her neck and elbows ached.

Walking with her sweet Jesus through the green fields of paradise. Hannah Bond clenched her jaw and whispered, "Maggot!"

The pain instantly left her neck and elbows, and she inched along the floor without pause for two more hours.

Either the cadet had done a good job, or there was nothing on that floor to begin with. Bond had pinched a few grains of unusually light-colored sand into a bag, but that was all. She stood and stretched. For another hour she glassed venetian blind slats up to eye level. Then she gently raised all the blinds to just above the wide wooden sills. She examined each sill as she had the floor and the slats. Through the front windows, she could see the sodium lamps of Wapanucka. When she finished a sill, she lowered its blind.

The last bottom rail clattered softly over its sill. Up in the darkness, a creature scratched at the rafters.

Bond did not pause. She walked quickly to the unlocked window, ducked under the blinds, opened it, and went out as she had come in, hands first. She turned and shut the window.

* * *

Thirty-five minutes later, at 1:10 a.m., Bond turned off Oklahoma 1 onto Greasy Bend Road. It approached the Washita River through thickly forested bottom. In the Buick's headlights, a fox loped across the road, its eyes briefly flaring.

As Bond rounded the last curve before the river, the bridge's trusses loomed over moonlit branches. No vehicles were parked near the bridge approach on either side. Bond parked under the bridge on the upstream side, screened from headlights coming either direction. She turned off the Buick's lights and watched the water's surface in moonlight. She could barely sense its motion. She knew that would soon change.

CHAPTER 30

When Hannah Bond aged out of foster care at eighteen, almost twenty years ago, she had a mental list of things foster parents had forced her to do that she would never do again. Noodling for catfish ranked high. One of her foster fathers—not the one who killed her little sister—took her, when she wasn't yet ten, to this very river, upstream near the Arbuckle Mountains. He made her strip to her undershirt and underpants and stand on the bank under an August sun while he swam and dived along the vertical banks, groping for catfish in submerged nests. He could hold his breath for more than a minute—enough to create suspense.

When he had pulled a fish from its nest, he burst to the surface, the cat bent between his fists. He inhaled loudly as he flung it to the flat bank near Hannah. Some of the fish were a yard long.

When he lurched up out of the Washita, his T-shirt stained mud-red and his hands bloody, he told her it was time she learned to help feed her family. She had not expected this. She was a strong swimmer, but the river bristled with snags and it was murky. She could not see where she would be sticking her hands. But she set her stoic frown and nodded once.

If she balked for an instant or looked him in the eye, her foster father would break a switch off a bank willow, pull it through his fist to strip off the leaves, and lash her back until she bled.

She swam beside him, on his left, across the river to the base of a stone bluff that cut the current a little. When they reached the bluff, he grasped her right wrist and counted down. They went underwater, their legs splaying as they pushed themselves down the submerged rock, half swimming.

Hannah felt him pause and push her hand into a horizontal cleft. The current dragged her hand slowly along the top lip of the stone. The cleft shallowed out; another opened just above it. She needed air needed air needed air. An image of the willow switch made it worse.

The fish struck her hand like a rattler. Hannah fought the urge to inhale, almost blacked out as her foster father wrangled the fish—and her—upward to light and air. The fish somehow released her hand as she broke the surface. She gasped and gagged, flailing at the river. He leg-kicked backward, flung the big cat onto the opposite bank.

Hannah stood in the shoals, her breath raspy, and let the blood-tinted water run off her fingertips.

CHAPTER 31

Bond had years ago removed the bulb from the Buick's dome and trunk lights. She had just grabbed her duty belt and opened the door when her cell phone vibrated. She retrieved it from the passenger seat and saw Maytubby's name on the screen. She shut the door.

"Awful late, Bill."

"It is, Hannah," he said softly. "Any luck at Alice's house?"

"Not a damn thing. Some white sand."

"You mean no blond hairs."

She exhaled through her nose.

"Are you back home?"

Silence.

"Where are you?"

Hannah stared at the river.

"Where are you?"

"Greasy Bend Bridge." She scowled at herself.

"I was afraid of that. Magaw would never let you check out a wet suit." Maytubby hung up.

"Shit," Bond said to herself. She tossed the phone onto the passenger seat, opened the door, grabbed her duty belt, pulled the unlit Petzl over her head, and walked around to the trunk. She flicked on the headlamp and pulled out her blankets and long underwear. The north wind had laid, and a light frost sparkled in the moonlight.

With her free hand, she threw the bundle of cotton over her shoulder and shut the trunk. She began to walk the bank upstream from the bridge, where the killer would have thrown the pistol. Only ten paces from the bridge approach, she struck thick underbrush that tugged at her freight. Bond twisted and bulled her way through brambles and scrub oaks to a place she judged that the weapon would have struck the water.

Here she stomped down a small clearing and laid her baggage on the earth. She unrolled the blankets, lifted two corners of the pile, draped the halves over low limbs; then she took some disposable gloves from her duty belt and pulled them on. The duty belt she covered with brush. She yanked off her boots and socks, shed her aviator hat, coat, shirt, and pants. She turned her head, and the lamp, toward the Washita. Here the bank was shallow but sinewed with roots. If the water was forty degrees, she had twenty minutes in it before she would forfeit her judgment.

She laddered down the roots and mud to the edge of the water. Here she turned off her headlamp, slid it over her head, and threw it onto the higher sand beach. She flat-dived into the river, keeping her head above water so she could pant against the shock. Seven or eight shallow breaths, then she dived to the bottom and sank her hands into the mud. She grasped the mud against the current, kneading it for the gun as she moved between the banks.

In the frigid blackness, she brailled empty shotgun shells, cans, bottle necks, coontail weed, fishing line. Her left hand slid over an object made of smooth metal and wood. She shot to the surface, panted. She heard the faint sound of a vehicle engine behind her and saw a brief sweep of light on the surface. When she turned in the water, still panting, the bridge was empty. She dived again. With both hands, she pulled it from the mud. By the time she had it to the surface, she knew that it was a hatchet. She flipped it onto the bank for the cold-case locker. Nobody threw a hatchet in the river for nothing.

Every ten seconds, she swam upstream to the surface, panted, and dived again. After four dives, she could sense the numbness advancing. But her sinuses throbbed. Some coyotes barked far downstream. She heard the willow switch smack her spine. And then James mocking Alice. She filled her lungs, bent at the waist, swam a few strokes upstream, went down again.

Hundreds of bottles. A submarine forest of bottles, their necks roped with waterweed. They must have been thrown far to sink and lodge here. She fingered them gently so the broken ones didn't cut her gloves. She couldn't hold herself against the current. When she broke the surface this time, she had to swim farther upstream.

At the bottom of her next dive, her numbing hands found a rock bottom swept clean by the current. Her noodling days now stood her in good stead as she found clefts and knobs by which to pull herself upstream and bank to bank. The difference was, now the rocks felt alien and distant, as if her hands were floating free of her body. Her grip was stiff and mechanical.

Rock gave way to less cluttered mud. Bond surfaced and dived. She could no longer knead the mud, only poke it.

Her eyes were shut, so she floated in darkness. She was suddenly aware of another darkness, this one invisible.

CHAPTER 32

Maytubby went back to Jill's bedroom to get his clothes. She breathed deeply under layers of blankets. The garage apartment was cold, though its floor furnace roared.

Light from sodium streetlamps fell through the living room blinds. Maytubby pulled on his civvies and buckled his duty belt. The room smelled like burnt pecans. Jill muted her phone at night, so he texted her: *"Hannah diving for gun at Greasy Bend. Bringing her hot coffee. Yeah, she'll spit nails. Also I stole your couch blanket."* The coffee part was a lie.

Maytubby took his magnetic portable cop strobe from the Ford's glove box and slapped it on top of the cab. He wouldn't turn it on until he was out of Ada.

* * *

The deer rut was two months past; bars had closed hours ago; the road was deserted. Maytubby pushed the big eight. Tommy Hewitt's death had put an end to his rule about never speeding.

Maytubby pictured Hannah in the cold river. What did Emily

Dickinson say about freezing persons? *First the chill, then the stupor, then the letting go.* Hannah would be the last person to let go, but she was human.

With the blue strobe shuttering on the scrub oaks flying past, Maytubby watched for a constable at every crossroads hamlet. If there was one sitting in a dark car, he gave the old Ford a pass.

CHAPTER 33

Rage and hunter's finger—the brief return of sensation and flexibility to chilled digits—did not buy Bond any more time in the water, but for ten seconds she ripped up Washita silt like a wild hog. She was setting her hands on the bottom to spring herself toward air when her right hand struck metal.

She burst to the surface and inhaled loudly. When she opened her eyes, she had a drunk's tunnel vision. She shut them and lashed the surface to defeat the current, sucked air, and dived again. The bottom was all the same here. She dug in the mud to keep from floating down. She needed air. She needed heat. Five seconds, ten. She breached again, crouped in air, and went down. This time, her fingers stiffening again, she found the steel, pinned it between her hands, and thrashed to the surface.

She rolled onto her back and kicked toward the bank. Her limbs and torso felt leaden. An owl glided low over the water, its moon silhouette edged in silver. She flung the pistol onto the bank.

When her back struck roots and sand, Bond scissored her legs and pivoted out of the water. She began to shiver violently, her teeth clattering. When she tried to stand, her knees buckled. She panted and spasmed, her cheek pressed into the sand. Her blankets were very near, but cold had driven all else from her mind. Her body curled of its own accord, and she pressed her forearms against her shins. She rocked herself.

The meager heat within her finally allowed her to open her limbs, get on her hands and knees, and summon an image of herself on the riverbank. Lifting and planting each knee and hand, she managed a wobbly crawl. When she reached the brambles, she was too weak to push them back. They raked her face until she broke into the little clearing she had made.

Here she dropped onto the flat part of her blanket stack and rolled so the hanging part fell over her, from her head to her feet. She rolled more and again let her body curl. But now she had insulation. Before warmth could reach her, Bond felt the cold blood in her limbs flooding into her core. She endured one last long surge of tremors.

Then she could hear again, even through the blankets. Small animals rustling in the brush, a bobtail downshifting on Oklahoma 1. Not long after that, as she warmed her hands in her groin, she began to feel them. They were sticky. She couldn't leave the blankets yet.

Bond heard the mumble of an engine, faintly at first, then distinctly. She shook her head in the blankets, steeled herself against Maytubby's aid.

The engine sounded close enough to be at Greasy Bend Bridge. Then it fell silent. Maytubby had likely driven the last half mile by moonlight. And he wouldn't slam his pickup door. She doubted he would call her name. She listened in darkness, gently flexing her limbs and breathing more slowly.

After a few minutes, she heard the twig-snap of footfalls—slow, halting. The sounds grew fainter and then disappeared. Minutes later, they resumed, this time growing louder. Soon, she could hear brambles scraping cloth. When the steps were very near, Bond said, into the blankets, "Bill."

Silence.

She heard a cell phone click and saw, through all the blankets, the glow of the phone's light. It brightened and dimmed, brightened again.

"Shit," she heard a man say. "He wasn't lying." His feet shuffled a little. Then he said, much louder, "What *is* this?"

She heard the rasp of a lighter and then smelled cigarette smoke.

The footsteps came closer, behind her, and then stopped. The kick hit her sacrum. She didn't expect the blow, which whipped her spine. She didn't groan or move.

"What the *fuck* you doing in that river?" he shouted. Not Richard James, not Roger Teague.

The footsteps circled her slowly. The cell light brightened and dimmed. The circle widened. She heard a branch snap and then sounds of flogged brush. Down her spine, a blade of pain swept the numbness away.

The flogging stopped, and the footsteps again approached. She sensed a body close to her, then felt herself rolling away from it, her warmth thinning as she spun until she lay on the leaves, blinded by the cell's flashlight. "Oh, for fuck's sake," he said. The cold embraced her once again, and she began to shiver.

The light played over her and the blankets. "I said, bitch, what were you *doing* down there?"

Bond stared hard at a spot just above the light, tried to grit her chattering teeth. "N-n-n-n-noodling, you pissant."

CHAPTER 34

Maytubby cut his headlights as soon as he turned onto Greasy Bend Road. Hannah wouldn't need any advertisement. Even before the bridge trusses appeared a few hundred yards from the river, he saw a light-colored pickup parked beside the approach. He didn't see Hannah's Buick. He parked, pulled on his camo hat, draped Jill's blanket over his neck, and began walking fast toward the bridge.

In the woods upriver from the bridge, a small bright light appeared, darting around before it disappeared. When it reappeared, this time unmoving, he heard a man shout something. Maytubby broke into a run.

The pickup, an '85 Chevy resembling one in the Sentinel lot, faced him, so he couldn't flick on the Maglite and get its tag when he passed it. At the edge of the approach clearing, the bosk was jagged shadow. The light was deep in there, and he was going to make a lot of noise getting to it.

Maytubby stopped to pull off his runners and socks, which he left there. He followed the edge of the thicket to the riverbank, slid down a few feet to a thin beach, and turned upriver. The sand was cold. A few roots the moonlight didn't reveal broke his jogging stride, but the low susurrus of the Washita masked the sound.

The man's "Fuck!" stopped Maytubby in his tracks and echoed from a taller stone bank upstream. Looking down, he saw where someone had come out of the river. As he turned to follow the track, he saw the moon reflected dully by a hatchet blade, and a headlamp. And then by a pistol. He didn't pause to pull the pistol from the sand. If Fuck Man hadn't found it, he likely wouldn't.

Maytubby could see the cell light clearly. It was aimed toward the ground. He stopped, drew his service Beretta with this right hand, and took the unlit Maglite in his left. He raised the pistol and the light together, his thumbs touching. He crept toward a tiny clearing. The phone light moved away from Maytubby. He seized the chance, walked quickly into the clearing, aimed the pistol at a dark figure, and flicked on the Mag. "Police!" he shouted. The man whirled and grimaced at the LED glare. This time, Maytubby saw the crooked, stained incisors of Duncan Calls. "Drop that phone!"

Calls dropped his cigarette and bolted from the clearing the way he had come. Maytubby raised his pistol above his head and lowered the flashlight toward Hannah Bond, who was again rolling herself in blankets, this time leaving her head out. He holstered his pistol, knelt beside her face, and leaned over. "You know how this is done," he said.

Bond opened her mouth and inhaled the warm lung air he blew into it. He smelled onions and Calls' cigarette. A vehicle engine came to life; its sound moved away from them. A few seconds later, there was the distant sound of breaking glass.

Soon, Bond's tremors stopped. Maytubby found her long underwear and clothes, laid them beside the blankets. She breathed slowly a few times, then barked, "Quick!"

Maytubby chose the underwear bottoms, dropped his flashlight, and stretched open the waistband. Bond rolled until she lay on the ends of the blankets, shucked off her wet bra and panties, and lifted her legs. She winced as she pulled the bottoms up. "That whoredog kicked me in the back." Maytubby grabbed the top and bunched open its hem and neckline while he took a step on his knees. He yanked the neckline down over her matted hair, and she got her hands through the armholes and pulled the hem over her breasts.

Maytubby scrambled to get her civvies, socks and boots, coat and aviator hat. When he turned his flashlight back on Bond as he handed her pants, socks, and boots, he said, "You cut your left hand."

She reached for the socks and pants. "Didn't know it until two minutes ago. Nothin'."

While she pulled on her socks and pants, Maytubby draped her coat over her shoulders and tugged her aviator hat over her ears.

"I look like Amelia Earhart?"

"If her plane had crashed in the Washita River. In winter."

"That wasn't James or Teague or the Volvo guy. Sulak. But you know that." Bond stood up to finish dressing.

"His name is Duncan Calls. He killed Tommy Hewitt at the Golden Play."

Bond paused in zipping her coat. She looked at Maytubby. "You ..." She lowered her head and shook it while she finished zipping. "Well." She cleared her throat, slid her feet into her boots. After flexing her hands a dozen times, she tied the laces.

CHAPTER 35

Jill Milton awoke to the frantic barking of her neighbor's border collie. The ruby numerals of her bedside clock read 5:42. She sat up in the chilly air and found Maytubby's message on her phone. His side of the bed smelled faintly of her sandalwood soap; the room, of burned pecans.

The dog slammed the chain-link fence, which shrieked against its posts. Jill pulled a flannel robe over her jersey pajamas and walked to the living room's front window. She lifted a blind slat and saw, by the light of a streetlamp, the roof and bed of a light-colored Supercab pickup parked in her drive. Her car was parked in the garage below her.

Her phone was on the bed. Before she got to the bedroom, she heard a vehicle door open below. Then another. She stopped in the short hallway and opened the closet door. Enough light filtered through the bathroom blinds to show her the barrel of her great-great-grandfather's 1915 Springfield double-barrel twelve-gauge shotgun. Her grandfather had taught her to shoot thrown bottles with it on the South Canadian. She reached into a box of 2¾-inch birdshot shells on the overhead shelf and dropped two in her robe pocket.

Pointing the gun at the hall floor, she thumbed the top lever and broke open the breech. The border collie snarled and barked. She took the shells from her pocket, slid them into the barrels, and closed the gun, which she balanced in the crook of her left arm. She retrieved her phone and said into it, "Call Ada police." As she walked into the living room, the dispatcher answered. Backing toward the wall opposite the front door, she gave the dispatcher the King's Road address and reported a suspicious person outside her garage apartment.

Her old wooden steps creaked and snapped. Dropping the phone into her robe pocket, she switched on a table lamp and leveled the shotgun at the front door. She took a step back with her right leg and set it. When the light came on, the snapping had fallen silent for a few seconds. Then it came in a flurry.

The door burst open. Jill flinched at the splinters but held her stance. She saw the work boot of a thick, bearded man follow the door, in the man's hairy right hand an automatic pistol raised to balance his kick. In the instant before she shot the leg he stood on, she saw his wide blood-shot eyes. The dim vampiric face above his shoulder was Rooster, the man who had wanted to call her a nigger. As the burly man collapsed, smashing her banjo, Jill raised the shotgun to the height of Rooster's face. He ducked and spun away. She heard him falling down the stairs.

An intact string on the banjo rang.

The heavy man bellowed from the floor but still held the pistol. Jill tilted the shotgun away from her face and struck his wrist with the butt. The pistol fell from his hand, and she kicked it away. She heard the roar of the pickup engine, the collie barking, and sirens whooping up Broadway toward King's Road.

Through the doorway, she could see the pickup—a Ford, now in streetlight—gain King's Road and accelerate westward. Covering the thick man, the shotgun's butt in her armpit, she called Dispatch, said she had shot an armed intruder and that he needed an ambulance. She added that an accomplice had fled west on King's Road in a light-colored Ford Supercab. The first cruisers appeared from the east fifteen seconds after the Rooster left.

CHAPTER 36

Maytubby took a paper evidence bag and disposable gloves from his duty belt and collected the filtered butt.

"Vehicle stopped on the bridge and shined a flashlight down here," Hannah said. "Whoever it was must have told Calls somebody was in the river. Gimme your light." Maytubby stowed the evidence bag and handed her the light. She found the pile of leaves over her duty belt and kicked them away.

"Calls didn't know you're a cop."

She handed the light back to Maytubby and buckled her belt. "I told him I was noodlin'."

"Wily."

"Snaggletooth has seen your old Ford. He'll call his friends, and they'll start puttin' two and two together."

"The pilot runner in Cache that shot my tailgate ..." Maytubby fell silent and stared at the ground. "He had fancy binocs in that plane, and he buzzed my pickup on his way east. If he talked to them ..."

Bond pulled off her aviator's hat and dried her hair with Jill's blanket. "Tell Jill I'll wash it and give it to you." She threw it atop her own blankets, glanced at his feet. "No shoes. I thought you didn't do that Mexican-running-Indian shit in the winter."

"Only when stealth demands."

Bond sighed as she replaced her hat.

"You found James' gun, Hannah."

"I found *a* gun, Sergeant. Let's not jump it."

"C'mon, let's get it bagged."

"You go put on your sneakers while I dig out some fresh gloves and get my headlamp."

"I'll bring the Ford to the bridge." Maytubby followed Calls' path back to his shoes. When he had them on, he ran down the dirt road toward his truck. Ragged clouds sped across the moon, and a rising wind moaned in the treetops.

In the beam of Maytubby's flashlight, broken glass glittered on the road beside the F-100. There was glass on the bench seat, too. He opened the cab door and shone his light on the headliner. The twenty-gauge pump was still in its rack. He swept the glass from the seat with the Maglite, got in, and drove to the bridge approach. He instinctively parked crosswise to his path back to Hannah. He pulled the twenty-gauge from its rack, then tilted the back of the bench seat forward and pulled out a half-empty box of birdshot shells. He took five and put the box back. As he walked toward Bond, he pushed shells into the magazine tube.

When he found her on the riverbank, she was squatting in the sand, her headlamp illuminating the pistol. She had a plastic evidence bag in her left hand, and a straight foot-long branch in the other. She lifted her head and blinded Maytubby for an instant before she looked down again and slid the branch into the pistol's trigger guard. Maytubby carefully laid the shotgun on the sand.

"Sorry. Man, a box would be a lot better than this derned bag." She handed Maytubby the bag.

"I'll call Scrooby."

"You do that," Bond said. She lifted the pistol, and lowered it into the bag. Maytubby sealed the bag.

"Fairly new Smith and Wesson M-and-P," he said. "No magazine, slide locked back, no shell in the chamber."

"Shoots a nine-millimeter Luger—same as the casing I found wedged up on the bridge."

"The nine ammo I found in the Cache plane was not Luger. Auto. No taper."

Maytubby held out the bag. Bond took it and inspected the pistol with her light. "Right," she said, walking a few paces toward the river, laying the bag on the ground, and piling leaves and brush over it. She jabbed a long limb into the ground to mark the spot. "Where'd you get that pump?"

"Roof rack in my pickup."

"Whoever saw me in the river scairt you?"

"Abundance of caution."

"Where'd you learn to talk like that? Shit, never mind. You saw the hatchet, too?"

"Yeah. You don't throw a good hatchet in the river without a reason."

"Good thing we grew up in the sticks." Bond found the hatchet. "You have a plastic bag in your belt?"

"Yeah, but only big enough to cover the handle."

"Hobson's choice. Probably been in there since statehood, anyway. Whatchu eat for supper?"

"Butternut squash and pecans."

"Figures." She reached in her jeans back pocket and produced some long, shiny packages. "Have a Slim Jim. Or two. I won't snitch to your girlfriend."

Maytubby took two, skinned the plastic off, ate them quickly, and pocketed the wrapping. "Thanks, Hannah." Bond polished off three and stuffed the wrappers in her empty coat pocket.

The first faint blue light of dawn unmasked the riverbank. A low rumble began from far away, approached fast. There was a loud boom, and the earth under Bond and Maytubby undulated. The river sloshed a little.

"Disposal well quake," Bond said.

"Coincidence, Hannah. Don't you read what big oil tells the papers?" Maytubby awakened his cell. "Jill called a little over an hour ago. No message."

"Late," Bond said.

"Or early." He was about to tap "Jill cell" in RECENTS when headlights swept the trees above the bridge. More headlights, followed by the low drone of engines. All coming from downriver.

Maytubby silenced his phone and put it in his pocket. He lifted the shotgun from the sand and brushed it off. "Let's get across that bridge before the Shriners get here."

Bond snapped the evidence bag off the hatchet handle, rolled off her gloves, and stuffed all the plastic in a shirt pocket. The hatchet she choked at its shoulder. Then she stuck the handle down behind the back of her duty belt, covering the head with her coat. The wood and steel hurt her back.

They jogged along the shore, then scrambled up bank roots to the higher ground, where their cars were parked. After they leaped onto the bridge's approach, they broke into a run. Under the trusses, the deck thumped with their footfalls. On the south bank, they jumped off the approach and ran into the underbrush just as the first vehicle rounded the last bend before the bridge.

"You think it's too soon to call for backup?" Maytubby panted.

Hannah said quietly, "It's too damn *early* to call for backup. At this hour, nobody but Eph on the beat in Tish. And calling Eph 'backup' is a stretch. Besides, maybe these folks are going to prayer breakfast."

"No Lighthorse down here … Renaldo's an early riser." Maytubby pulled out his cell and touched the screen. There was one bar. He held the phone to his ear. "He knows the lay of the land better than the rookie trooper on shift in Troop F." Maytubby stared at the ground, then watched through the trees as several pickups parked on the side of the road, behind his Ford, and others crept onto the bridge. "Hey, Jake …"

While Maytubby was telling Renaldo to come to the bridge along

the Washita's south bank, across the bridge from the approaching vehicles, Hannah moved her phone around until she had a bar, and then
called Johnston County Dispatch.

They put away their phones. The tinny drawl of a small engine
approached the last curve, and a yellow motorcycle emerged from the
trees. The rider was not wearing a helmet. His blond hair glowed in the
cloudy dawn.

"James," Hannah said.

"The welder's Bronco is there. Looks like Crum's ninety-one Ford,
blue Dodge Dakota from Powell Road, Calls' eighty-five Chevy."

"And that damn Jeep!" Bond said. "His ironed pants is going to get
dirty."

"I figured Teague to be back in New Mexico by now."

"Here comes the silver Volvo. Sumac." Bond paused. "Sulak."

There were no more headlights in the trees. "We're missing the
Supercab Ford with the monster grille."

"Still a circus without the elephant."

The sky got no brighter after dawn; the clouds sagged. The wind
wheeled around to the north and swept sleet over the bottomland.

"You got a speed loader on your belt for that old pistol, Hannah?"

Bond grabbed a pouch on her duty belt. "One."

Maytubby nodded. She'd had to be nimble with the loaders in the
timed CLEET exercises. Everyone else in her cohort had an automatic.

CHAPTER 37

Jill Milton could barely hear the cries of the wounded man on her floor. She had almost forgotten the temporary deafness that set in after a quail-hunt shot. The small room had amplified the sound. And it had that almost-sweet putrescent smell, like the artesian fountain at Sulphur. Through the smoke haze, she saw blood spatters on the door frame and rug.

A patrol officer stepped into the doorway with her pistol aimed at Jill. "Lay that shotgun on the floor and step back from it."

Jill looked at the wounded man and said, "Yes, Officer. I need to take one step back before I lay it down, to keep it away from him."

"Okay," the officer said. Her name badge said O'KEEFE.

Jill took a step back and laid the shotgun on the floor.

A second Ada cop appeared behind O'Keefe, his pistol, in both hands, raised in the air. He surveyed the room and holstered his weapon. While O'Keefe kept her gun trained on the wounded man, the second cop patted him down and removed a subcompact revolver from an ankle holster. He slid it aside and handcuffed the wounded man. "Can you get me a towel?" he asked Jill.

She went to the hall closet, took out a folded bath towel, walked into the living room, and tossed it to him. He wrapped it around the leg wound and applied pressure as sirens whooped up Broadway from downtown.

Jill's knees trembled. She looked at her wrecked banjo, its worn Mylar head spattered with blood.

CHAPTER 38

One by one, the doors of the pickups on the bridge and down below opened, and figures emerged in the dim light. Some held pistols, some long guns, all pointed upriver. Figures on the bridge walked out on its decking to the rusted iron railing beneath the larger truss beams. Those below walked slowly toward Maytubby's pickup, their firearms out. The blond man dismounted his motorcycle and took something from his saddlebag.

Maytubby thumbed his camera to video, zoomed the image all the way, and pushed the red button. His battery was at 50 percent, so the video was brief.

Someone on the bridge shouted to the men below that nobody was behind the Ford. They moved more quickly toward it. Two stopped behind its tailgate, and one pointed to it.

"They did talk to the pilot," Maytubby whispered.

One man discovered Bond's Buick, shouted something to the others, who briefly trained their guns on it. All the men on the bridge except Richard James leaned over the rail and looked down. James, who, they could now see, was carrying some kind of short rifle, walked across the deck to the opposite railing and stared downstream.

"Thinkin' about what he done," Bond said softly. "I could kill him right now." A crow cawed in the wood. Suddenly, she rose. Maytubby raised his free hand and said, "Hannah!"

She turned away from James and faced upstream. She had a baseball-size cobble in her hand. Reaching back, she took a step forward and hurled it with a grunt. She resumed her squat and watched the rock fly across the river and into the woods near where she had found the pistol. They heard the brush give when it landed, and so did the posse. James came across the bridge and joined the men who were jostling south to get a better view of the river bend. They were pointing toward the noise.

The riverbank contingent climbed down onto the narrow beach and walked upriver, their guns pointed into the woods.

"They're going to see that stack of blankets," Maytubby said.

"And take no pris'ners."

One of the front two men on the river lunged to his right and began firing into the brush. His companion came around to the shooter's left and followed suit. There were eleven shots. All the men on the bridge ran north, toward Maytubby's pickup, spilled off the approach, and turned upriver.

"Shall we, Hannah?"

Bond was already on her feet when she said, "'Fore they find the dead blankets."

They kept their heads turned toward the men's backs while running down the dirt road and up onto the bridge deck. They sprinted behind the trucks. Bond pushed over the yellow Suzuki as she passed. It thumped the deck like a drumhead. Coming down the opposite approach, they lost sight of the men. Maytubby shifted the pump twenty-gauge into his left hand so he could get to his truck keys. The shooting had stopped.

When they reached the truck, Bond scissored into the bed and drew her revolver. Maytubby opened the cab door and laid the shotgun on the floor, facing away. Its buttstock rode the transmission tunnel bump. He pulled out the manual choke and cranked the starter. Just as the big eight rumbled to life, the welder slewed up the muddy bank. The gray light fetched his gray eyes, and his long sandy hair, freed from the welding hood, fanned in the wind. Through the Ford's broken window, Maytubby heard him shout, "Here!"

When Maytubby ducked behind the dash to grab the pump, the welder fired three shots through the intact side window of the Ford's cab. When he paused, Bond brought up her revolver in both hands, rose on her knees, dropped the blades of her hands onto the bed's panel, and shot him in the chest. As she fired, Maytubby reached through the driver's window and twisted the side-view mirror downward. Then he rolled out of the cab with the shotgun and slammed the door. Sleet hissed against the Ford's old steel. Maytubby raised his head and looked through the ruined windows. The fat, drunk Powell Road guard appeared next, struggling up the lattice of roots. When he found solid ground, he gaped at the body in the dirt and looked around, confused.

"Police! Drop your weapon!" Maytubby shouted, bracing the shotgun on the Ford's hood. The guard seemed confused, began firing in the air and cursing. He staggered a few steps and fell on a heap of Greasy Bend trash. "*Uuuuugh,*" he moaned. And then he was quiet. Maytubby and Bond could hear him rasp above the river sound.

A third form materialized from the sleet, also unsteady as it clambered up the bank. He was wearing a bright orange watch cap over long, stringy hair. And orange socks. He waved a pistol uncertainly as he squinted against the sleet.

"Lon Crum!" Maytubby yelled. The man halted. "Police! Drop your gun and run! You do not want to die for these worthless bastards!" A few more shapes appeared far behind Crum, who immediately did as he was told, dropping his pistol and lumbering past the Ford down Greasy Bend Road. Maytubby pulled his shotgun off the hood and ducked behind the Ford.

A burst of what sounded to Maytubby like machine-gun fire came from the river. He heard *thok, thok, thok,* then crashing brush, a cry, and a thump from where Crum had gone. "Bump stock," Bond said from the pickup bed. Whoever fired it was lying prone on the beach, shooting over the bank. "I'm coming over," Bond said just before she pivoted over the panel on Maytubby's side of the truck. She quickly rose in a crouch, wincing at the hatchet in her waistband. As the barrage resumed, clanking against the pickup, they each planted their feet behind one of the Ford's tires. Some of the rounds kicked up dirt under the truck. "This Ford is about to look like Bonnie and Clyde," Hannah said.

Indistinct voices and snapping brush came from the river. The bump-stock fusillade stopped. Maytubby bent and looked into the side-view mirror. The prone man was rising, and two men were duck-walking on the beach toward him, holding pistols. One was very tall. The other was Duncan Calls.

Hannah was watching Maytubby. "Smart," she said.

Maytubby rose and threw his pump on the hood. He fired at the bump-stock man, ejected the spent shell, and fired at the tall man before taking cover again. A cascade of single shots struck the Ford, but the bump stock was silent. Bond rose above the panel and emptied her revolver at stooped forms. When she fell into a crouch, she snapped open a pouch on her duty belt, released the revolver's cylinder and ejected the casings, took out a speed loader, inserted the cartridges, and flipped the cylinder shut.

Maytubby checked the mirror. It had been hit by a bullet and gave him only a kaleidoscope—several images of each man in thin triangles. One man staggered away. The tall man was in a crouch behind the riverbank roots. Calls had disappeared.

Another series of semiautomatic shots struck the Ford. "Yeah, yeah," Hannah said. "You feelin' those Slim-Jims, Bill?"

"I am, Hannah. Manna from heaven." He fell prone on the ground and fired two more shots from the twenty-gauge before scrunching up behind the front tire. He was answered by a dozen more pistol shots— quick but, by their frequency, from a single gun.

Maytubby glanced up at the mirror and saw, in two of the triangles, an Oklahoma Highway Patrol car inching along Greasy Bend Road from the south side of the bridge. "Renaldo's here," he said to Bond.

He looked in the mirror again and saw another man crabbing toward the tall man. "We have a new shooter, Hannah."

"Yeah, and where'd Snaggletooth and Richard go?"

"Good question."

They both spun around to search the road and woods. Nothing. A loud barrage from the river erupted, and they turned to face it. Maytubby took a knee at the front fender and fired his last round from the shotgun. He dropped the pump and drew his Beretta. Bond stood up and spent three of her speed-loader rounds on two scurrying forms.

Maytubby saw multiple tiny Renaldos advancing with their rifles down Greasy Bend Road. The trooper knew Maytubby's pickup and would size up the situation without help.

"Stay where you're at!" The voice came from behind Maytubby and Bond. "Drop your guns! Hold your fire over there, Teague! It's Rick. I got 'em."

"Shit," Bond said into the truck panel. She and Maytubby threw their pistols out.

"Stand up, put your hands on your heads, and turn around."

They did as they were told. Sleet spun around the golden visage of Richard James. He had the bump stock of an AR-15 assault rifle snugged against his shoulder, his right hand tight around the rifle's pistol grip, its barrel pointed at them. He let his left arm dangle.

"Well, if it isn't Bumfuck's finest," James said. "An Indian cop and a cracker bitch. Where'd you get that policeman belt, big sister?" He extended his left arm and made a fishtail gesture with his hand.

"Why'd you kill her, James?" Bond said flatly.

He dropped his free arm and chortled. "You know my name. Huh." He squinted. "Oh, yeah. The amazon speed-trap deppity. Small world. Well, Ms. Lang saw me with my boss at the fried-pie Sinclair station in Davis."

"You get the fancy hooch for doing that?"

James blinked and shook his head. Sleet stuck to his hair. He put his left hand on his hip. "Damn. Really." He laughed. "No, big sister, the Blanton's is nice, but I got a lot more than that. Somebody told me you were in that river last night. You said you were noodling."

Behind James' left hand, Bond and Maytubby saw someone in a crouch, walking very slowly toward them on Greasy Bend Road. The shape slowly picked up speed.

"I somehow doubt that. If you don't tell me where the gun is, I'll gut-shoot you and the Indian and leave you to shit yourselves to death. If you do, I'll kill you clean. First this world, then nothing." James paused. "What're you looking at?"

"Just your sorry ass," Bond said. She and Maytubby recognized Eph a second before he fired his pistol. The round clanged into the Ford, barely missing Bond, and James spun around. As he unleashed a burst of automatic fire, Bond found the hatchet head under her coat and pulled it from behind her duty belt. She grasped the bottom of the handle as her noodling foster father had taught her with a stump for a target, leaned back like a pitcher, and launched the hatchet firmly but gently so that it spun end over end. The blade lodged in James' right shoulder. His rifle spattered fire into the earth as he fell.

Bond and Maytubby retrieved their pistols and ran toward James. They heard, behind them, the boom of a big rifle, then a smattering of bump-stock and pistol fire, then another boom. Eph ran toward them, waving his pistol. "I got 'im!" he yelled. "First shot!"

When they met over James, who was bleating on the ground, Eph gestured at the hatchet with his gun. "What the hell is that?" he said.

"Holster your gun, Deputy," Bond barked.

Eph frowned and did so.

"You saved our lives," Bond said to him.

Eph's eyes widened. He said, "Really?"

"Get his rifle and take it back to your cruiser," Bond said. "Make sure the safety's on, keep your finger out of the trigger guard, and point it away from you. Check on that guy you passed in the ditch. Call ambulances from Tish and Ardmore.

Bond stared at the hatchet. "I should pull that thing out and let you bleed out. I ain't your big sister, either. I *was* a big sister once. Before a jackal like you killed her. That was the word you used, right?"

James writhed and sobbed.

"Hannah," Maytubby said, "I'm going in after Calls."

"Yeah," she said, holstering her revolver.

More whip cracks from the river. Maytubby ran to the edge of the brush and used his gun and free hand to part brambles and oak saplings. This time, he couldn't silence his movements.

There was no need. Even before he gained the clearing, he could hear Calls grunting and panting. Maytubby stopped and watched as he pawed at the earth beside the stack of Hannah's blankets. Even as sleet sifted down through the trees, the man's sweatshirt was soaked with sweat.

"Duncan Calls!" Maytubby said, training his pistol on him, "You're—"

Calls flipped in the dirt and reached for his holster. Maytubby stomped on the hand and set his pistol against Calls' throat. "We have James' gun." Maytubby pulled Calls' pistol from its holster and threw it into the brush. "As a citizen of the Chickasaw Nation, you are under arrest for assault and eluding a police officer." Maytubby recited the man's rights as he lodged his Beretta under Calls' skull and pinned him to the ground. "You want to sell me a coffee machine?"

There were shots in the distance.

"This was not some Circle-K grab-and-go in Moriarty, Calls. You killed the father of two little girls. For what? Some fistfuls of casino cash?" Maytubby grabbed his collar, pulled him up. With his left hand, Maytubby took plasticuffs from the back of his duty belt; then he pulled Calls' arms back and fastened the cuffs on his wrists. "Walk," he said.

When Maytubby and his prisoner gained the clearing beside the bridge approach, Renaldo was marching a tall man in cuffs, at the point of a pistol, up off the beach onto the bank. Renaldo carried a rifle in his left hand. "Bill. Hannah." He nodded. "How'd you guys draw a damned army down here?"

Sleet now poured over Greasy Bend in wind-driven whorls.

"It's a big outfit, Jake," Maytubby said, squinting against the ice. "Robbery, drugs, embezzlement, blank-receiver guns."

Renaldo and Maytubby ordered their prisoners to kneel. "I thought there were three bodies," Renaldo said, "but one was a passed-out drunk. I moved his gun a little farther out of reach. Can you watch Slats here while I radio Dispatch for the medical examiner and OSBI? I'll pick up the drunk's gun on the way.

"Sure. Thanks," Maytubby said.

As Renaldo jogged across the bridge toward his cruiser, Hannah said, "I got a nice, warm ride back to Mercy in the ambulance. You got a long, cold wait for the bureaucrats. My back hurts like a son of a bitch."

The sleet changed to snow, which grew on the grass and limbs, silencing the bottomland. Maytubby and Bond stood still, exhaling clouds of vapor.

The roar of a big engine approached from the east on Greasy Bend Road. They turned and watched for the ambulance from Tishomingo.

From the snowfall emerged a large white pickup with a big pipe grille. It was coming fast and showed no sign of slowing.

"Got-*damn*," Bond said. She grabbed James by the belt and dragged him to the far ditch. He cried out like an animal. "Is there no end to these turd-knockers?" she shouted, as she unholstered her revolver.

The other captives looked up as the truck approached. Maytubby raised his Beretta in both hands and aimed at the driver. The pickup slid to a stop. Maytubby recognized Rooster at the wheel. The man's little eyes menaced the scene only a second before he raised a pistol, not at Maytubby but at the kneeling tall prisoner. His first shot and Maytubby's, both through the Supercab pickup's windows, were simultaneous. The tall prisoner fell backward. Taking Maytubby's round, Rooster jerked to his left, recovered, and swung his pistol down toward Calls. Maytubby and the Rooster again fired at once. The Rooster's shot struck Calls in the chest, and Maytubby's hit the Rooster's right shoulder.

The Rooster pitched over on the bench seat, both shoulders bleeding. His pistol fell on the floor. Maytubby and Bond ran to the pickup, pistols in hand, and flung open its opposite doors. The Rooster, his thin head bent, was heaving. Maytubby stared into the tiny yellow eyes. The

Rooster coughed up a laugh. "Nobody left to squeal like a pig."

"Maybe," Maytubby said as he took the shooter's gun.

"He's a ugly bastard," Hannah said.

Ambulances from Tish and Ardmore moved up Greasy Bend Road from opposite directions as Renaldo ran back across the snow-covered bridge. As he approached the pickup, he said, "Who the hell is this?"

"The next-to-last player," Maytubby said. "Whoever owns this truck, which was the getaway at Golden Play, and the vehicle that—"

"The railroad killer," Renaldo said.

"Yeah," Bond said.

"He's the last one," Maytubby said.

"Troop F had news on that," Renaldo said. "Woman in Ada shot a home intruder. An accomplice fled the scene in a truck like this. 'Bout half an hour ago."

"Jake, can you cover my prisoner and this guy?" Maytubby said.

"Yeah."

"I'll go back to James," Hannah said.

Maytubby had to walk to the middle of the bridge to get a signal bar on his phone. When he called Jill, she picked up just before voice mail.

"Are you okay?" he said.

"Who told you?"

"Renaldo. Baby, are you okay?"

"Baby? You never …"

"Jill?"

He heard her inhale deeply. "Yes, Bill. I am pretty much okay. The other guy is not okay, but he is alive. The police and EMTs are here."

"The freedman's Springfield?"

"Yup. I'm pretty shaky. And freezing. I'm in my robe, and the front door is still open. There's snow blowing in. How …" The connection died.

Maytubby walked in circles until he got a bar on the phone. When Jill answered, he said, "Hannah is fine. She dived in the Washita until she found a pistol. She was cold as a corpse when I got here. But she brought lots of blankets. Said to tell you thanks for yours."

"She's welcome. Officers, can I go get a coat?"

Maytubby heard one of them agree. After some seconds, Jill said, "There. Much better. And I think I need gloves."

"Jill, listen, the guys in cahoots?"

"Yeah?"

"All but the two who visited you came to see Hannah and me on the Washita. There was an ugly episode. Some people are dead."

"*Episode*? Oh, God. What a word."

"Hannah is accompanying one suspect in the ambulance to Tish. I have to wait here with Renaldo until the medical examiner and OSBI get here. Might be an hour and a half before I can leave. You want to go somewhere else for a while?"

"No. I'm not superstitious. But I am going to finish that Viognier. Fry an egg. I'm told I can't 'disturb' the crime scene. The wine and egg won't do that, you think?"

Maytubby heard the sangfroid return to Jill's voice. "The Rooster came here from there," he said. He's also alive but out of commission. You shot the kingpin, you know?"

"The big hairy guy the EMTs are lifting onto a stretcher just now?"

"That guy."

"He fell on my banjo and busted it."

"The evil that men do after you've taken them down."

"I'm getting the wine, baby. And I'm taking the day off."

"Be there in a couple of hours."

Maytubby hit the red button on his cell and looked down from the bridge. Snow was bleaching the corpses. The muddy Washita creased its banks like blood on a starched sheet.

CHAPTER 39

Snow whirled into the cab of the F-100 as Maytubby pulled the hand choke and started the engine. It had been photographed, measured, and dusted for so long, Maytubby had to call his fiancée to tell her he'd be late. He surveyed the hive of law enforcement vehicles and bustling forensic troops from OSBI, the knot of remote television news trucks with their antennas raised as high as they could go, swaying in the wind. Even Johnston County sheriff Magaw had made an appearance. Maytubby had declined all media requests for interviews. Scrooby and Magaw had not.

Maytubby waved at Renaldo and a couple of Highway Patrol officers from Troop F. He moved the column shifter into first and inched down Greasy Bend Road. The drive on Oklahoma 1 to Nichole Hewitt's house in Mill Creek took fifteen minutes. Maytubby squinted against the wind and snow.

His teeth were chattering when he pulled into the Hewitts' driveway, his pickup crunching pecan hulls as it neared the house. Before he could open the door, Nichole, her mother, and the girls filed out the front door, wearing winter coats and Sunday shoes. The girls wore short coats, under them long dresses.

When Nichole saw Maytubby, her swollen eyes widened. She turned to her mother and said something. Her mother ushered the girls back inside.

Maytubby got out of his truck. Nichole hugged her coat and came down the steps to meet him. They embraced in the falling snow and then stood apart. "Bill, what happened to your truck?"

He looked toward the house and then exhaled, lowered his head, and shook it. "Tommy's funeral!" he said.

"Yeah," she said, pulling her coat even tighter. "Ten o'clock. What happened to your truck, Bill?"

"I'm going to miss Tommy's funeral," he said. His eyes smarted. "I'm so sorry, Nichole."

"What happened?"

Maytubby wiped his nose with his coat sleeve. "The gang who robbed Golden Play? There was a firefight down by Ravia early this morning. This is no time to burden you with details. But the man I believe shot Tommy was shot and killed by another member of the gang."

Nichole grimaced and sank her chin into her coat. "It's all so horrible," she whispered.

"Yes. It is. His name was Duncan Calls. A Chickasaw citizen and a crook who had lived out of the state a long time. OSBI is at the scene, collecting evidence."

Nichole kept her head down and reached for Maytubby's arm. "Thank God you're not hurt," she said. She withdrew her hand, raised her head, and looked him in the eye. "We have to go," she said.

He nodded. "Hug the girls for me," he said. He looked around. "And Jill ..." He wavered. "... has come down hard with the flu."

Nichole was weeping when she turned her head toward the house and nodded.

Maytubby watched her mount the steps. He got in his truck and drove toward Ada.

CHAPTER 40

Maytubby and Jill hugged on the tiny landing where the stairs going up to her apartment made a right angle. Jill had changed into blue jeans and a gray cable-knit sweater. They kissed a long time, rocking a little.

Jill said, "It seems like weeks since we burnt the squash." Snowflakes melted on her black hair. They hugged again. "Mmmmm …" She jerked her head back. "Shit! The old Ford! I didn't see it. What the Sam Hill happened down there? It doesn't even have a windshield!"

Maytubby, still holding her, turned to regard the truck and then looked back at her. "More important than that is what happened in your apartment. You are strong. But being awakened in the night by a man who breaks down your door. And then having to shoot him to save your own life. That's ugly."

"It was."

"And I didn't see it coming. Didn't think the pilot of that dubious Cessna in Cache might glass the Ford's tag. Or that he might have a mole who could run the plate and tie you and Hannah and me together with online news stories about the Hillers mess at Nail's Crossing last summer. I'm sorry, Jill."

She smiled weakly. "Can you call me 'baby' again? It was so not like you."

"I love you, baby."

"Ah-h," she sighed.

"Badass," he growled.

She nodded. "Today."

They exhaled together, the vapor of their breath trailing over the banisters.

As they turned and walked up the second flight, Maytubby said, "I stopped by Nicho … the Hewitts' house in Mill Creek."

Before they opened the splintered door, Jill stopped and faced Maytubby. He said, "Nichole and her mother and the girls were leaving for Tommy's funeral."

Jill gasped and put her hand to her mouth. "Oh, God. I …"

"It's okay. I told Nichole you had the flu. She'll learn the truth when it needs to be told. Her mother took the girls inside before I told her that the man I think killed Tommy—his name is Duncan Calls—was shot and killed by one of his own gang down on the Washita this morning."

Jill grasped Maytubby's coat by its lapels and gazed into the falling snow. "It was cold comfort," she said.

"Yes," he said. "We know her well." They stood very still for some minutes, the thick snow falling.

"Let's go inside," she said.

CHAPTER 41

Ten days later, on a sunny Saturday, Hannah, Maytubby, and Jill slid into a leatherette booth at Polo's Mexican Restaurant on Main Street in Ada. The place was crowded at noon. Hannah and Maytubby, both off shift, wore civvies—Hannah a denim shirt and denim jeans, Maytubby a pale-blue oxford button-down shirt and beige corduroy pants. Jill wore blue jeans and a black turtleneck sweater.

A server brought them waters and started to hand out menus. Hannah held up her hand and said, "We been here before. We know what we want. I'll have steak fajitas. She," she said, pointing at Jill, "will have cheese enchiladas. This guy"—she pointed at Maytubby—"will have all the beans and rice and guacamole and lettuce and stuff that comes with my order. I just want the meat. They"—she waved at Jill and Maytubby—"don't take much to meat." She winked at Maytubby. The server nodded and scurried away.

Hannah narrowed her eyes at Jill. "I hear you shot Bluto in your living room with your great-great-granddaddy's old Springfield twice-barrel."

The server brought a basket of chips and some ramekins of pico sauce. Hannah dug in. "Good for you," she said, gnawing a chip. "Made that bastard eat his vegetables."

Jill closed her eyes and nodded.

Hannah sat back and frowned. "At the graveside, we put Alice's ashes not ten feet from that old racist Governor Alfalfa Bill Murray, if you can believe it." The table went quiet, only kitchen sounds in the back.

"Now, Sergeant," Hannah said, "I didn't want to hear from Scrooby—least of all from Magaw—what-all has happened since the shoot-out at the bridge. I told them all I'd wait and hear it from you." She folded her arms across her chest, closed her eyes, and leaned back in the booth.

Maytubby tapped his nails on the table. "Jill has heard all this—and that Pitts stove in the door of my house just before he went to her place. So. You remember the ugly guy," he said to Hannah. To Jill he said, "The Rooster. The guy I shot in the cab, said he had killed everyone who would squeal like a pig?"

Hannah kept her eyes closed and nodded.

"He squealed—on his boss, Bluto, the guy Jill shot. The boss' name is Jared Pitts. Pitts drove the white pickup in the Golden Play robbery. He controlled the whole Sentinel Vending shell company that ferried drugs and blank receivers all over southern Oklahoma and north Texas. OSBI raided the Powell Road compound and the Gill Janitorial office at the airport. ATF stormed the white-supremacist encampment in Paris. The night before the raid, the Nazis shot up an empty Hispanic church, Puerta del Cielo, outside Paris, with bump-stock rifles."

The fajitas arrived on a cart pushed by a server. She poured vodka from a portion cup over the meat and set it aflame with a long barbecue lighter. When the fire died, she used potholders to move the metal-in-wood plate to the table. Then she served the other dishes.

Hannah did not move to eat but remained with her eyes closed and her arms across her chest.

Maytubby looked at his vegetables. "OSBI found that Pitts managed James' money. They have the torn glove you finally gave them,

Hannah. They recovered James' prints on the pistol you found in the river. Cold river water preserved the oils. And their ballistics team matched the bullet they recovered from Alice with the gun. Also, your cadet found a blond whisker in Alice's house before you got there. The pilot from Cache remains at large."

"Go on," Hannah said.

"Teague, Sulak, Calls, the welder—I don't recall his name—the tall fellow, whose name was Dorko, and Lon Crum all died in the gunfight. The drunk guard from Powell Road is in Johnston County jail, as you know, Hannah. The FBI, back when they didn't know a Chickasaw had killed a Chickasaw in Indian Country, looked into Calls' computer and found an Amazon receipt for a batch of temporary tattoos, including the satyr tat Calls was wearing when he shot Tommy Hewitt."

Hannah still sat with her eyes closed. "And Richard James?" she said.

"He's in OU Med Center in Oklahoma City, charged with first-degree murder in the death of Alice Lang."

Jill and Maytubby looked at Hannah. She opened her eyes. "Pitts?"

"Also in OU Med Center, charged with first-degree murder in the railroad killing and with many other federal charges."

"I hate to say it, but Scrooby did the Lord's work." Hannah unfolded her arms, took her water glass in hand, and raised it above the fajitas. "Here's to keepin' the powers of darkness at bay."

Maytubby and Jill raised their glasses.

After they drank and set their glasses on the table, Hannah said, "I'm starvin'. Let's eat."

ACKNOWLEDGMENTS

I am deeply indebted to my gifted editor, Michael Carr, whose skill and cheer go above and beyond.

Warm thanks to my wife, Karleene Smith, for detecting vague passages in the first manuscript.

Jason O'Neill, former Chickasaw Lighthorse chief of police, patiently explained the basics of tribal jurisdiction. Any errors on this score are mine alone. Staff at the Lighthorse Police have answered my telephone queries in helpful detail.

My dear friends Sarah Miracle and Jill Fox supplied details about nutrition education. Jason Eyachabbe introduced me to the Chickasaw language and demonstrated the rudiments of stickball. Cody Dixon was a thorough guide on our tour of the Kullihoma Grounds.

Warm thanks to others who commented on the manuscript: Jim Rosenthal, Mary Bess Whidden, and Desiree Hupy.

Robert Kelson and Paul Swenson, both retired law enforcement officers, answered my amateur's questions patiently. They did not begrudge my poetic license with police procedure.

Drs. Michael and Myrna Pontious graciously provided medical observations.

Thanks to Danuta Press, who presided elegantly over the Norman roll-out of *Nail's Crossing*.

I am indebted to Jon Portis for discovering a crucial plotting flaw in *Nail's Crossing*.

A warm salute to Jenny Vigil, the owner of Norman's Gray Owl Coffee, and to the shop's crew of brilliant baristas, who daily solved vocabulary and diction puzzles: Laney, Laura, Andrew, Rachel, Chris, Braden, Roshni, Erica, Katie, Boob, Emily, Avery, Caleb, and Lucas. Also to Dr. Mark Norris, the Owl's resident linguist, and to its genii Dale Wares and John Green. Thanks as well to the baristas at Michelangelo's: Sierra, Reese, Marla, and Carolina.

Debbie and Lee Maytubby (no relation to our detective) supplied me with a relation's history of the Chickasaw Nation.

Many thanks to my agent, Richard Curtis, to my Blackstone publicists Lauren Maturo and Jeff Yamaguchi, and to my cover designer, Djamika Smith.